MAKARA

a novel

KRISTEN RINGMAN

Handtype Press
Minneapolis, MN

ACKNOWLEDGMENTS

Excerpts of the novel have previously appeared in slightly different versions:

Deaf American Prose: 1980-2010 (Kristen Harmon and Jennifer Nelson, editor; Gallaudet University Press): "Torn."
Eyes of Desire 2: A Deaf GLBT Reader (Raymond Luczak, editor; Handtype Press): "Darkness."
Lotus.zine: "Prologue."
Pitkin Review: "The Moon."

Handtype Press, LLC
PO Box 3941
Minneapolis, MN 55403-0941

www.handtype.com

The publisher is grateful to David Cummer and Wesley J. Koster for their invaluable assistance with this project.

Printed in the United States of America
ISBN: 978-0-9798816-4-0
Library of Congress Control Number: 2012943678

A First Handtype Press Edition

FOR
MY OWN "NEELA"
AND MY LITTLE SEAL, RÓNÁN

Makara:

A Sanskrit word for a mythological water creature,
sometimes seen as a selchie or half-seal.
Linked with Lakshmi, Hindu goddess of prosperity, and
Ganga, Hindu goddess of rivers.
Connected to the Hindu elephant-headed god, Ganesh.

It is also described as a hybrid or monster
(between forms, neither one thing nor another);
a form that is half-animal and half-fish.

In Old Greek, the word means "blessed."

IRELAND

Island: in the shape of a dead man, a prophecy.

Seal mother: enveloping me, human skin, seal skin.

Distant father: whiskey on his breath, already a tragedy.

Stranger: framed in grey rocks, darkening sky, my youth
decaying.

AN FEAR MARBH

The waves crash against my ankles in the dark as I walk down the length of the beach. I've just returned from my annual swim out to *An Fear Marbh,* the island that has always reminded me of my father. I can reach it because my mother is a selchie, a woman on land and a seal in the water. She's given me webbed toes and fingers and the ability to swim underwater for long periods of time.

Not everyone believes in selchies here, but I have a friend from our hometown, Tadhg, who also had a selchie wife like Father. They had been unable to bear children, so after Tadhg's wife left him to return to the sea, he was never able to fish in these waters again. He drives all the way to *Trá Lí* to fish now. All Tadhg has left is me, and I don't visit him as much as I should. It's too painful for me to be here.

It's been a decade since Father died but when I return here, to the place where I once saved his life, I can almost feel him as I swim through the eelgrass down below.

Sometimes Mother follows me underwater. I can feel her seal eyes on me, but I don't approach her and she doesn't approach me. She knows I blame her for not saving him.

Father was a biologist, but deep down he was an aspiring novelist. His last and only manuscript had been written just before his death. I've been sitting on it for ten years, unable to read it. On this trip home, I will finally write down my story before reading his for the first time . . .

SEAL MOTHER

During the summer when I turned eleven, Father and I took the ferry to *An Blascaod Mór*. We did this every summer, but this was the first time he told me his version of the story of how he met Mother.

We walked along the shore of the beach near the place where people used to live many years ago. The ruins of various homes were scattered across the hills. He turned to me and pointed at the far end of the beach. He signed in Irish Sign Language, *That's where I met your mother.*

Mother had told me the story countless times, but I wanted to hear it from him. His story. Mother had told me that he didn't like to remember it correctly. His scientific mind wouldn't allow him to see it as it really happened. I waited for him to continue.

She appeared suddenly one night when I was alone studying the seals. I was walking down the beach when I saw her. She was naked and I thought she was crazy. Crazy and beautiful. She spoke a language I didn't know, but she stayed with me. She told me this island was her home but she loved me. That's why I bring you here every year. I'm hoping she will appear again and come home with us.

Father turned from me as his eyes filled up. I found myself wondering if he really did believe that Mother was a selchie. He must have seen her skin, I thought. He must have wondered how she could have suddenly appeared with no clothing. And how did she get her seal skin to our mobile home?

We kept walking, hand in hand, along the beach. Father didn't look at me for a long time. Questions burned inside me, but I didn't ask them. Sorrow clammed up his hand until his skin felt sticky and gross, but I couldn't let him go. I followed his gaze as he scanned the crashing waves, searching for grey seals, searching for her.

❧

Until I was six, Mother was a tall, slim woman with long black hair that reached her waist. Her name was Brannagh. It meant a beautiful woman with hair as dark as a raven. Her eyes were deep brown and her skin sparkled with the brine of the sea even when she didn't swim. She spoke Old Irish that Father strained to understand. I learned to read in Irish earlier than any of the other kids in our village because of her. I was born deaf and Mother had accepted it. She learned Irish Sign Language and taught me how to read and write in Old Irish as well as English before she left us and returned to the sea.

Mother and I learned ISL from dictionaries before I was able to learn from a visiting teacher of the deaf in school. Father was never able to sign as naturally as Mother. I remembered the argument my parents had about where I would go to school. Their faces contorted in anger as they shouted at each other but I couldn't understand.

Mother told me later: *We decided to send you to a Hearing school in An Dangean. A Deaf teacher will visit and help you there. Your father feels better sending you to a place with Hearing people, not just Deaf people like you. He also works in An Dangean and the Deaf School is farther away. Are you ok with this?*

I could tell she didn't agree with Father, but I understood later that she had to listen to his wishes because she knew she was leaving us. I was too young to comprehend what mainstreaming would mean. The isolation. The staring. The comments mean kids wrote to me on blackboards or small pieces of paper, their laughing eyes. Kind words from teachers or other students didn't always console me in Mother's absence.

Mother often brought me to *Tráigh a' Choma*: a tiny cove amidst the high cliffs that overlooked *Na Blascaodaí*. A yellow stretch of perfect sand between clusters of giant dark grey rocks. When the tide came in, the sand disappeared. We rode bicycles there and had picnics at the far end, away from the tourists. Even though the tide was strong, Mother taught me to swim there. If I ever got nervous or pulled away by a wave, I'd find myself in her arms in a flash. Her body never looked as strong as it was.

Sometimes Mother would stare into the breaking waves as if she was searching for something. I always asked, *What's wrong, Mummy?*

Memories, just memories, she always replied. Then mischief would replace the far-off sadness in her eyes, and she would tickle me so that I couldn't ask her anything more.

Before she left us, we were drawing in the sand on the beach. She picked me up and held me so tight it hurt a little. She signed, *If you're scared or you need me for anything, come here or to the rocks near our home, ok?*

But why? Where will you be? I signed, but she answered my pleas with a slight shake of her head. No more questions.

The next day, I woke up and felt a strange emptiness in the mobile home. I felt the vibrations of Father pacing on the other side of the wall. I walked out of my room, Father stopped in mid-step and looked at me with red-rimmed watery blue eyes. I knew she had left. I ran back into my room to dress.

When I opened my door fully clothed, I ducked past Father and ran outside. I knew he was yelling or trying to follow me, so I hid behind the other mobile homes in the park until I reached the rocks and the small beach. I scanned the horizon, looking for her hair, her body, something, anything.

An animal scream burst from my mouth: "Muaaaaaaaaahhhhhm!"

My tiny hands and feet scrambled over the rocks. I was crying. I slipped and fell a couple times. The knees of my jeans became dark circles of wet cold. My fingers turned pink. I had gone far down the beach, over stretches of rocks, before I was too tired to continue and fell down upon a large rock and sobbed.

I jumped when something large climbed up onto the rock. I sat in wonder as a grey seal leaned towards me. The eyes staring into me were so deeply familiar that I reached out and stroked the thick slippery skin. The seal moved and suddenly the skin on the top of her head parted open and a human head of messy black hair emerged. The seal's deep brown eyes were now framed by the perfect wet face of Mother. She slowly pulled her arms out of the seal skin so that its whiskered face was stretched across the middle of her chest. I stared.

She started moving her hands: *This body is mine. I live in the ocean now because I have to. I'm not leaving you. I love you. Because of this body, I can't live on land anymore. It's not your fault. It's because of my body. Do you understand?*

I screamed again. I have vague memories of my arms flying, hitting her blubber. Digging. Trying to pull her out. Pull her back, but I was too small. I couldn't really hurt her skin or her body, but in her eyes, in their tears, I saw that I was hurting her inside. That stopped me. My arms hung loose at my sides. I screamed again: "Muaaaaaaahhm!"

She reached out and pulled me into her. Her large seal body below me, human arms around me. I cried and cried until the seas within me were dried up until they flowed out into the seas within her.

I ran down to the rocks every day to see her. Every day she climbed up beside me and pushed halfway out of her skin to hold me in her arms. I never told Father. He wouldn't have believed me. Father the scientist. He couldn't fathom that she could be a seal and a woman. I blamed him. I thought that if only he had believed in her, she would be able to stay with us forever.

When I was eight, I read about the myth of the selchie. A fisherman would steal the seal skin from the selchie in order to make her live with him for seven years as his wife. I learned that one of their children was usually the one who returned the skin to the selchie so that she could return to the ocean. I hadn't done that and Father didn't seem to believe in any of this so I was confused as to how Mother ended up with us and how she managed to leave us. One afternoon when I was with her by the sea, I stole her seal skin.

Fionnuala, what are you doing? She signed with a slight tremble.

I'm a fisherman and I'm stealing your skin! You can come back to me, now, right?

Her face sank and she took me in her wet arms that smelled of salt and fish. I held her slippery skin tightly with both hands. I knew I had her. I wouldn't let her have her skin back and she would have to come back. Home. Father would stop hiding in his room with his books. He would stop going to the pub every night. He would be happy and I would be happy and—

I looked up at Mother and she had tears in her eyes. I let one hand go in order to say to her, *You don't want to come home? If I take your skin, doesn't that make it easy for you?*

She looked at me. *The story doesn't work that way. You're not a fisherman. I loved your father and I chose to go with him. He never stole my skin because I hid it myself. And yes, it was for only seven years. I can't come back again. I wish it was possible, but I have to live in the sea now. Do you understand?*

I shook my head and clutched her skin. I could taste the salt of my own tears in my mouth. I didn't understand why we couldn't change the story again if she changed it already. I didn't know that no myth was set in stone. That the power of legends lay in their ability to change. I held her skin tightly until the sky grew dark. She kept her arms around me, too. I held her skin until my hands hurt. I thrust her skin at her and slipped out of her grasp. I climbed up the rocks to the road as fast as I could. I didn't look back.

SEPARATION

Summer Solstice: I was ten. It had been four years since Mother left us. The sun had set, and the moon was rising above us like a giant lamp in the sky. I had ridden my bike in secret to *Tráigh a' Choma* to meet her. A group of seals were bouncing onto the sand as I tiptoed down the curved road to the beach. The moon on the wetness of their skin made them shine like black gemstones. I rushed the rest of the way down and sat against the bottom of the cliff on a rock to watch. Mother told me to be discreet. She would tell the others at the right time. I had never seen another like her. I felt my own skin hum and tingle as the skin of the seals parted at their heads and the women slipped out.

They had long tangled hair, slim bodies, small breasts. Each brought her skin over to the same rock where they left them, like giant strips of seaweed in a pile. At the sight of so much nudity, I almost looked away, but they started dancing. It was as if their long limbs were meant to move in wide arcs, kicks, leaps. They twirled and swayed, each pose a work of art, each gesture as clear as a sign. Their bodies were strings on invisible harps. The white curling waves behind them pounded like drums. Their hair fanned out like notes.

I had never seen such raw beauty, such sound. I felt it through my entire body. My blood pumped with the beat of the waves. My limbs wanted to stretch and arch as theirs did. I wanted to sing with my hands, but the words to their tune were like the stars above me. I could see their forms. They were there—in the sky. But I couldn't pull them down. My hands couldn't mimic their language, but I could read it and through my own skin, I could hear it. In their movements, I saw what Mother's human body was for. I saw why she belonged to the sea, her orchestra. She looked human, but she never was. She wasn't a seal either, but she was an extension of the glistening curved lines of the water.

Gradually, they slowed down. Tears pulled at the edges of my eyes as their song came to an end. Light as wind, they smiled and pranced over to their skins and wiggled back into them. As Mother reached for hers, her eyes staring into mine, another hand snatched it away. I leaped to my feet as she looked up to see her captor. Father. I was frozen by the intensity of their exchange.

The other seals scattered and bounced into the waves while my parents stared into each other's eyes. Her skin hung like a dead, shrunken seal in Father's guilty grasp. Mother's hand still in its reach towards it. Her hands moved first: *My Ruarí, please. Let me be who I am.*

My eyes opened wide. She was signing. Her lips didn't move. She must have wanted me to see. She was using her private name for Father that meant *red king*, for his red hair. My heart fell open and broken in the sand at my feet. I didn't want to feel anything anymore. But I couldn't hold Mother back.

This is what you left me for? But you're my wife!

Father's body swayed as he signed. I could smell a hint of whiskey in the wind. He must have been at the pub down the road. In his glazed eyes, I could see his disbelief. I could see his mind struggling with the vision before him. He couldn't fathom it, even when he held it in his hands.

I tried to tell you. I'll always love you. I gave you as many years as I could, but I don't have any more left. I need you to let me go.

Drops shimmered down the sides of her face. Her body swayed in the breeze until she allowed herself to fall into Father's arms. Behind the watery film of my tears, I watched them rock each other. Arms encircling each other's bodies. Bare skin against cloth. Her skin hanging down behind her like a blanket I wanted to steal and wrap around myself.

Father's body sank down to the rocks as she slipped out of his hands with her skin. His eyes never left the sand where her feet made their last footprints and traced them to the place where she slid into her skin and bounded into the empty waves. It wasn't until she was gone that I crept over to him and placed my own smaller body in his arms. We fell asleep there. My body was sore from the roughness of the rocks beneath us when I woke to a bright sun and Father still in his slumber behind me.

He and I never spoke of that night. For years I was convinced he didn't remember it. Not until I was a teenager.

During the months of spring after I turned twelve, the wind blew so hard from the sea that it swept people off their feet. I used to go out for long hikes along the rocks alone. I needed caves and hiding places everywhere because I wanted to be anywhere but home.

The man seemed nice at first. He was from somewhere in Europe and had been staying in our village for a few weeks. He kept to himself and rented one of the holiday homes by the sea. I never knew his name. His hair was dark and his eyes a cold shade of blue. I had only seen him from a distance, walking by the sea or along the road towards the pub. The accent on his lips was as unfamiliar as the way his hands pinched my skin until I bruised.

I hadn't sensed his footsteps on the rocks behind me. I was wrapped up in the motion of the waves far below, searching for Mother a bit later than usual. The sky was already dark. I knew I should have given up and gone home. I could barely climb along the rugged terrain. The sea was full of shadows. The hand was fast as it grabbed my body from behind. I was pushed down against the rocks. They weren't small enough for me to lift and smash into him. As I felt him ripping my pants down, I rose up out of my body. I needed to be removed. I was not the one being violated. I was not the tiny girl barely discernable beneath the large man as he pushed and pushed until she seemed to have fallen into the cracks between the rocks.

When I couldn't see her anymore, I panicked. In a swell of energy like the waves below, I pushed him off her and plummeted into the gap between the stones. He nearly lost his balance. I might have been able to push him into the ocean, but I had to save myself. I let the rocks squeeze me and I pushed as far back into the cliff as I could. I barely noticed the scrapes along my arms. I could see him reaching, but I had squeezed back so far into the gap between the rocks that he couldn't touch me anymore.

The man gave up and fled. I believed I was the only one in the village to remember he had ever been there. It took me an hour to get out of the crack between the stones. I sat on the cliffs with the darkness wrapped like a cloak around me, swearing silence. I couldn't possibly translate such an experience into language. As I ran my fingers along the sharp edges of the gap in the rocks that saved me, I knew that space would remember. The event was branded on the stones. I never returned to that place.

The residue of him was so overpowering that I didn't question why Father suddenly wanted to leave Ireland. I watched him explain that there was a great scientific opportunity for him in Indonesia. I could spend a few years in South India with his friend's family, and wouldn't that be an amazing experience? India? India meant nothing to me. I didn't even care that we would be leaving the only place where I could see Mother because I couldn't tell her what happened. It would've been hard to tell her anything else.

I

N

D

I

A

Shadows: crawling over buildings, misunderstood, feared, black.

Rough skin: grey elephant trunk, reaching down, painted white lines.

Bats: furry, brown, up-side-down, quivering unused wings, suspended.

Goats: crooked silhouettes climbing red rocks, hooves catching on tree roots.

Coconut: milk spilling over mouths, thick meat sliding to the dirt, dogs receiving.

ARRIVAL

Father held me by the hand. His hands were pink like the Irish, even though he grew up in America. He was Irish enough to be pink-skinned. His faded brown beauty marks looked like splattered dirt. His red hair was barely long enough to be pulled back into a short ponytail. Stray curls escaped it and hung down along the sides of his face, one of his hands continuously tucking them behind his ears. His blue-green eyes always seemed full of sea dreams. I felt safe when his hand wrapped around mine. He would lead me through this strange country.

The airport in Madras. Black and brown skin. Signs with names held up by taxi drivers. We found ours—O Shay—printed incorrectly but distinguishable. The sign was held by a short brown man with a black moustache. He wore a white shirt above tan suit pants above rubber sandals different than any I had seen before—with a circular loop around the big toe and a strap holding down the foot. I kept my dark blue eyes down and my hands hidden beneath my bags when he looked at me. His mouth moved strangely and his head wagged side-to-side. Father was smiling as they spoke and shook hands.

The air was filled with dust and black clouds. I coughed a few times. Musky perfumed incense mixed with fuel oils. People were everywhere, hanging out of buses and tiny rickshaw taxis that were like golf carts with bright yellow hoods. We took one of those. Father wanted me to have the real India experience. I didn't really care. Either way the curvy green hills and rough blue seas were gone. I was squished into the back of a taxi with our bags while Father sat in front and talked with the driver. We sped through the wide city streets past bicycles, motorcycles, mopeds, buses, rickshaws, and cars. When I saw the goats, dogs, cats, or cows on the sides of the roads, I smiled.

I have always loved animals. They spoke to me differently. I didn't need to read their faces to understand what they wanted or felt. I read their movements. The tilts of their heads. The ways their bodies arched towards or away from each other told stories I could not translate. Mother taught me how to sit close to the animals and be invisible so that they could be themselves. I learned sheep first because they were all over our fields by the sea. They feared everything except the uneven ground beneath their feet. The animals there and their stories that I could peel open made me realise that I could exist without her. Mother spoke through them.

Father turned back to me as we pulled into a bus station. His hands moved in awkward yet quick ISL: *We get out here now.*

Ok. That's fine. I answered with one hand gripping the black edge of the driver's seat in front of me as we stopped short.

Father looked thrilled through the sweat that poured down the sides of his face. His eyes gleamed with a mix of excitement and nervousness that I had never seen before. I knew he hadn't been to India since before I was born, but he had an obsessive fascination with all things Indian. Old photos from the 1970s filled our home in Ireland: Father smiling beside his Indian fisherman friend, holding up the fish they caught, painted cows, stretches of empty beach, close-ups of the strange blue circular plankton that washed ashore. But I didn't want to think about that. Instead, I climbed out of the taxi and into a bus. Our T-shirts stuck to our skins as women wrapped in rolls of fabric eyed me suspiciously.

The bus quickly filled up with people, and I was pushed close to the window as we began to move. Father's tall, lanky body separated me from the masses. The ride was different once we left the city. The air became cool as we got closer to the sea. Villages along the left side of the road blocked my view, but I knew the wide stretch of blue waiting behind them. Father had shown me maps of where we would be going.

I wanted to see the ocean, so I made the villages disappear in my mind and watched the white-capped waves crashing upon long sandy beaches. Forests of palm trees grew on the other side of that stretch of sand where I could run unbridled, wind in my hair. Trees would be arched on one side of me; waves pounding on the other. Eyes closed, I leaned out the window to feel the wind's fingers on my face.

Eventually the bright white of the temples and the flashes of colourful statues of gods and goddesses crawled under my eyelids. I could see them like glowing particles of light through the dark of my closed eyes. I also liked the way the cow's horns were painted blue and red and yellow. I wanted to see more animals—elephants, monkeys, and tigers—but Father told me they were all in the north, except for the elephant in the city of Pondicherry. It was always in chains. I didn't want to see that elephant. The ride passed by so fast I could barely remember anything specific. Village after village, statues, animals, and temples, bodies moving on bikes or legs. We arrived at our destination exhausted. Father knew the white house with the rooftop that held *Ammā*, Neela, and her brother Mathi. Their father had died only four months before. He was a fisherman who taught Father how to fish the Indian way, and that was how Father came to bring me there—to that family who would become my own.

Nobody spoke of Neela's father, and Father never told me anything. I imagined he had a lot of trust in this family because he was leaving me with them for such an extended period of time. He loved Ireland but I had felt him getting restless before he even knew it himself. He had the ocean inside him, too, but I don't think he ever understood it the way I did.

We spent a few awkward days together. Father, myself, Neela, *Ammā*, and Mathi. People stared at us because we looked like a half-white and half-Indian family. Secrets were not kept easily in a village like ours. I learned to wear *punjabis* and the half-saris that younger girls wore. I felt less of an outsider. Neela was kind from the beginning, but her older brother was mischievous. Mathi's name meant the moon and also intellect. He stole my shoes the first day we arrived and it took three days for Father to find them. Mathi continued to play tricks on me. Their names, both having to do with the moon, came from their father's love and respect for the tides of the sea. His fisherman life was built around the moon's pull on the tides. I felt I could fit in with this family. They were ocean people like us.

Father left in a hurry. He had a boat picking him up from the southernmost tip of India, and he would go to the islands east of Sri Lanka, and then beyond to Indonesia. He said it was the trip of a lifetime. He also said he was leaving because he never felt he could care for me as well as Mother did. After she left us, I disappeared into the rocks by the sea. Father disappeared into himself and his scientific facts that did not shift like the ocean. He needed the constant. The definite. The straight line leading somewhere logical. But I was not that way at all.

After Father left, Neela, Mathi, their mother, and I took a bus inland to a place where a temple rose out of hills covered in white ruins. Monkeys lived there. They tried to steal food right out of our hands. We walked over the hills for a long time until I felt sweat running down my back. Neela and I stopped to braid each other's hair. This was the first time she touched me. I remember it now because of how her touch had changed over time. Back then her hands were in my hair, on my back, and I barely noticed. I was too busy taking in the surrounding stones, wandering Indian tourists, and monkeys eating the lice out of each other's hair. Neela's hands held no magic. They were the hands of another child. Her hair was pretty. I smiled at her shyly, making brief eye contact, and quickly looking down.

An astrologer lived in the desert-like hills, past the ruins of the temple, past the clans of monkeys, past the ragged green trees that looked like they were dying and screaming all at once. Neela, Mathi, and I stepped gingerly into the tiny hut behind *Ammā*. The man wore an orange lungi that I later realised was a costume of sadhus, or holy men. He wore clear crystal prayer beads like the god Shiva. I stood off in a corner as *Ammā* and the astrologer talked about me. I wished Father hadn't told her my birthday or the time I was born. It was embarrassing, and I couldn't even understand what they were saying. Mathi looked at me with a smirk. His eyes were laughing as I looked over to Neela and watched her eyebrows push together as she said something to hush her brother. He rolled his eyes at both of us and began investigating the hut. There really wasn't much there except for stacks of stray papers, books with Tamil letters that looked like curved doodles to me, and many crystals scattered on a low table. I liked the colours of them—clear, purple, orange, bright green, blue, and yellow—but I didn't know any of their names.

The interview seemed to go on forever. I wished they had let us play outside. Eventually the man sat down on his singular green mat in front of his table. He shuffled through papers for a while before he looked up and told *Ammā* something. She looked at Neela, and they both looked at me and smiled. I raised my eyebrows and had to stop my hands from signing *What? Ammā* gave Neela a pen and paper from her plastic woven basket-purse. Neela wrote down LAKSHMI, and pointed to me as she showed me the paper. The astrologer had given me a new name.

She wrote out something and showed it to me: LAKSHMI IS THE GODDESS THAT IS GOD VISHNU'S WIFE. SHE IS FOR WEALTH AND FORTUNE, BUT WHAT IS FUNNY IS THAT SHE CAME OUT OF THE SEA, AND YOU ARE LIKE THAT. THE MOON IS HER BROTHER, AND MATHI'S NAME MEANS MOON! ISN'T THAT GREAT? YOUR NAME IS VERY STRONG AND VERY PERFECT FOR YOU. WE ARE ALL HAPPY.

I looked at the smiling faces of Mathi and *Ammā*. I panicked and grabbed at the pen. BUT ARE YOU SURE I SHOULD HAVE THIS NAME? I wrote, my hand slightly shaking. I didn't want another name. I had always been Fionnuala.

She responded with a graceful hand and in perfect English: YES, OF COURSE. THE ASTROLOGER GAVE US THE FIRST LETTER – L – AND WE HAD TO THINK UP THE NAME, BUT HE AGREES IT IS THE BEST NAME. MANY PEOPLE HERE ARE NAMED AFTER THE GODS. IT IS LUCKY.

I was nervous but I relented. I knew a lot of people were named after gods and goddesses in Ireland, too. As we walked back to the town, I looked at the ground moving below me, thinking about my new name. Maybe it really was mine. I certainly didn't feel like Fionnuala here. By the time we reached the bus that would take us back to our village, I felt changed. I felt like Lakshmi coming out of the sea into a new name and a new life. It was like a skin I could shed, and I smiled because it reminded me of Mother.

My first days in India passed slowly. I felt lonely because nobody could understand my signing, but then again, not many people could.

Neela and I slept in the same room as the *puja* area. It was a tiny alcove in the wall where they had pictures of Ganesh, Lakshmi, and Shiva. At different times of the day, *Ammā* and Neela would prostrate before it and take some of the bright red saffron powder from the tiny bowl in front of the pictures. They placed this powder in a dot on their foreheads. The place of the third eye. Inner sight. I understood it because I always felt I had inner hearing. I could sense people's feelings. I wasn't sure if all deaf people adapted this way—listening for the words people aren't saying by reading their bodies.

Some days Mathi came and drew three white lines across his forehead. But most days he forgot or avoided it. *Ammā* used to drag him over to the puja space and thrust the little dish of white powder towards him. I watched his face change so fast. His ever-present smirk vanished when he applied the powder, as if he were working a spell upon himself. It fascinated me. His eyes looked far away towards something none of us could ever see. Once the powder was on and *Ammā* placed the dish back on the shelf, Mathi was himself again. He winked at me and ran off into the trees behind the house. He had that freedom.

Neela and I often had to help *Ammā* with the cooking and housekeeping. My favourite times were when *Ammā* allowed us to walk to the village to buy food. The goats moved down the dirt streets in packs. The parallel rows of shops each had their own wide blue tarp covering their baskets of fruits and vegetables. Little bags of nuts and spicy dried noodle snacks dangled from the overhangs. We always tried to save enough rupees for one of them, but *Ammā* didn't like us to snack too much.

I preferred the coconuts. I loved to drink them before the juice was sucked away into the white hardness of their ripened meat. *Ammā* gave us ten rupees a day for a coconut, because she thought they were healthy. All I knew was that they filled you up with thick milk and a hint of sweetness. I liked it when the shopkeeper would take an axe and crack the coconuts open so that we could peel out their juicy meat and let the pieces slide down our throats after we finished drinking. Sometime the pieces slipped out of their shells and fell to the red ground, giving us an excuse to lure one of the underfed street dogs over to eat them.

I went to school with Neela and began learning Tamil. Thankfully we were both twelve and able to attend the same class. She acted as a tutor for me since the public school didn't have sign interpreters, and I didn't want to travel three hours for the deaf school in Madras. Father had heard that they would probably try and teach me how to speak or read lips, and I didn't want to do those things. We settled on me attending the regular school with Neela helping me by letting me follow her notes, and I would try and teach her ISL so we could communicate more easily. If I had an interpreter in the classroom, I'd have to learn the local sign language at the same time as our subjects, which would have set me further behind in school.

Neela was as excited to learn ISL as she was to teach me Tamil. She had me practice drawing the 247 curvy characters that were combinations of letters hundreds of times. I couldn't believe that when two letters stood next to each other, they changed each other's shape. It was an impossible system to grasp. I became entranced by their curves and I was able to draw them all, even if I could not read their meanings. Tamil taught me that languages could be artwork woven across the page. Tamil words had countless meanings. A full explanation of each word could take a paragraph or an entire page. It reminded me of the Old Irish Mother used to write. I knew I would eventually learn all the old meanings for our Irish words, but Father pulled me away before I could. I didn't want that to happen in India. I wanted Father to wait until I had learned enough. I would force him to stay away. I was already starting to feel stronger.

At times, though, I got scared. I wanted the cool breeze of my Irish home, its cliffs, and the wide muddy fields of long green grass. Whenever I felt uneasy here in India, I went to the bathing room in the back of our yard. When I first arrived, *Ammā* showed me the place so I could have my first bath with buckets of heated water. As she opened the door, I raised my head to see a dozen dark brown bats fly into the far corner where they could hide between the top of the back wall and the roof. I had never seen bats before. After that, I found a way to open the door slowly enough that the bats didn't move. They remained hanging from the ceiling like toys rather than real animals. I sat on the stool and watch them as they slept. Beneath the cluster of bats, I felt safe.

I was on my way to the bathing room the morning Neela got her period for the first time. I had known older girls in our town in Ireland, so I knew what periods were. Mother explained them, too, because she didn't want me to be afraid when I saw the blood. The door was ajar and the bats had flown to the far corner. I pushed the door in slowly. I was afraid to find *Ammā* or Neela crying. Neela was huddled against the mud brick walls in the far corner. She looked relieved and scared at the same time when she saw me. I made sure nobody was around outside and gently shut the door before I approached her.

What's wrong? I signed hesitantly. Neela had picked up a lot of signing in the past few months but I always had to sign slowly to make sure she understood.

I'm dead. She signed back with eyes wider than I had ever seen them before.

How are you dead? I asked.

She was frustrated. *I'm not dead. I mean d-y-i-n-g.*

But how? Why?

She looked guiltily downward. But it wasn't until she pointed and spelled out *b-l-o-o-d* that I finally grasped what had happened. I signed, *Oh, that's your period.*

She looked at me without knowing what I was talking about.

I gave up the signing. It was taking too long and she didn't know every word yet, so we always had to spell things out and I wanted to make sure she knew what was happening.

I took out the pen and paper I always carried and started writing: YOU HAVE YOUR PERIOD. IT'S WHEN A GIRL BLEEDS FROM HER VAGINA ONCE A MONTH. IT WILL HAPPEN EVERY MONTH UNTIL YOU ARE OLD. IT MEANS YOU CAN HAVE A BABY.

She stared at me open-mouthed and started crying. I wasn't sure what to do next. I couldn't believe *Ammā* had never warned her.

It's ok. I tried to hug her, but she pulled away and curled up into a ball. She was shaking.

I didn't know how to do what Mother had done for me. I didn't know how to talk about our bodies when I barely understood it myself. I hadn't started bleeding yet. I sat for a while with her before I left to tell *Ammā*.

Neela grabbed my arm, signing, *No no no no no no, don't tell mother! I'll get some water for you, ok? Do you want some clothes, too?* I lied.

This calmed her enough to release her grip on my arm. She backed down against the wall and nodded. Her hair fell down into her face as she continued to cry. For the first time, I thought she was beautiful. I wanted to hold and comfort her, but we had never hugged before. Scared to touch her in a new way, I left.

I did go and find her clothes and a glass of water but I also found *Ammā*. She was immediately suspicious and began asking me where Neela was through her mimed gestures. It wasn't difficult to understand her made-up signs. Her eyes were so demanding at times that I wanted to hide because I never knew exactly how to please her. Her eyes never smiled. I led her to the bathing room, ducking into the doorway first to sign, *Sorry, she caught me*, before *Ammā* could enter. I dashed away.

I didn't know where to go, so I climbed up the steps to the rooftop. Sometimes we slept up there when the heat below was too much. It was nice with the stars glowing above you. In the heat of the day it was uncomfortable, but I still liked to watch the people and animals moving through the streets. I sat up there until Neela came out of the bathing room in a different shirt and skirt, though she still had tears on her cheeks and messy hair. I watched her being led slowly towards the small hut on the side of our yard. *Ammā* led Neela inside it and shut the door behind her.

I ran down the steps and rushed towards the hut. *Ammā* roughly caught me before I could push my way inside. She shook her head frantically. I looked into her hard eyes and saw the glimmer of a smile. This scared me more than her usual lack of smiles. *Ammā* dragged me back to our room and put me in bed as if she knew it was the only place I'd want to go. I hid beneath our new blue sheet with the white and grey elephants that walked across it. I tried to breathe in the scent of Neela through the fabric. I began to cry. I hadn't cried since I was in Ireland. I was ashamed but at least nobody could see me. I planned to plead for Mathi to help me, but what could I say to him? He was a boy and he would never understand. He would probably laugh at me. This made me cry more. I was really alone, and I couldn't even get up to go and sit with the bats that protected me and gave me strength. Eventually it was dark, and I fell asleep without even seeing the plate of food *Ammā* had brought into the room for me. By morning, the plate was covered in tiny red ants and I had to dump the rice and sauces outside.

Neela never came out of the hut. It had been days. I couldn't go to school because Neela was the one who helped me. Nobody else could do it, and I think *Ammā* must have known that because she didn't try to make me go. She was busy as usual around the house, and she kept bringing food and clothes to Neela, but it didn't make me think what she was doing was right. Mathi never went near the hut, but he also avoided me. It was strange because he usually teased me. He always laughed when he was around me. Now he was avoiding my gaze and running off even when I tried to get his attention or write something to him.

Finally, when I was moping on the back step, I saw the door of the hut open. I stared at Neela as she walked slowly to me. She looked stronger and more serious. Her hair was pulled back from her face and her half-sari was a solid dark red. She stopped in front of me and stared into my eyes before she smiled and hugged me for the first time. We were both awkward and pulled away fast. She saw the questions in my eyes and the fear in my face, and she laughed at me. She signed, *I'm ok. Mother said I'm a woman now. I can wear a sari and get married! I'm going to have a big ceremony soon!*

What?! But you were in the hut for days! Why? And aren't you angry?

She smiled again and tried to sign, *It's n-o-r-m-a-l because it's the first time I am b-l-e-e-d-i-n-g. Mother said I had to stay there.* Her head wiggled from side to side as she signed, *Only this time, I won't need to go in the hut ever again!*

I gave up trying to comprehend. Neela was back and she wasn't mad at me. Of course, Indian traditions were different from what I had learned. I wanted to understand, but I was exhausted at the prospect of Neela having to write it all out for me, so I decided to let it go for now.

Neela tried to change the subject. *Will you teach me some more signing now?*

Yes, of course. I signed back and we sat down on the steps until *Ammā* made us go and help with dinner.

Everything resumed after that day. It was as if Neela had never been away. Mathi went back to teasing me but he kept his distance from Neela. Months later the day of her ceremony began. It was announced throughout the village with large tan cards and fancy Tamil writing in red and blue. There was a tiny illustration foreshadowing the event of a woman in a yellow sari sitting down before a plate of fruit offerings with a woman on either side of her handing her gifts.

I helped *Ammā* set up the huge tray of fruit on an altar on the side of a giant room in a hotel that she had rented for the occasion. Huge bowls of towering mounds of the bright red saffron powder and other orange-yellow mounds of turmeric were set up as well. They looked like termite hills. Neela was petrified. We dressed her in a bright yellow sari with gold and white ribbon trim that made her shine like an Indian Goddess. *Ammā* gave her more jewelry than I had ever seen one person wear: rows of gold bangles ran up her arms, huge gold earrings in her ears, heavy gold necklaces, and a large gold flower nose ring. Her hair was plaited in hundreds of tiny white jasmine flowers tied together on a long string, and clusters of another pink flower I didn't know the name of. The long plait of hair and flowers hung thickly down the centre of her back to her small waist. It looked so heavy I wanted to hold it up for her, but *Ammā* wouldn't let me.

A man resembling the astrologer came in before everyone else arrived to go over the ceremony with Neela and *Ammā*. He wore a white lungi tied loosely around his waist and a string of clear crystal beads around his neck. His long greying hair was tied back with a black string. I stood slightly apart and watched them speak rapidly back and forth, wagging their heads from side-to-side. It made me dizzy after a while so I sat down and waited.

Neela was so quiet I thought she had gone mute like me. She stared into space. I wished I could sign with her, but I felt that it was the wrong time. *Ammā* would probably yell at her. I kept my hands down and wondered where Mathi was. Neela had said he couldn't come in until the guests began to arrive. I looked out the window at the sun setting into the green of the woods in the distance. It illuminated the red hills of the canyons. To my left, I could barely make out the horizon line of the sea and rows of palm trees beyond the village. I wished we had the ceremony on the beach instead of the big empty room with walls painted in bright blue. I looked down to see mopeds, rickshaws, bicycles, and crowds of people on foot arriving. The room wouldn't be empty for long.

Half an hour later the scent of the patchouli incense was so strong I coughed a little as I sat close to the altar with Mathi beside me. *Ammā* stood in the back of the altar with a bowl of deep red saffron powder in her hands. The man in the white lungi sat beside the fruit at the front of the altar and waved the burning incense sticks around. People filled the entire room behind me. Neela walked out, her feet weighted down by the thick gold of her anklets, her body slowed by the weight of her hair. Or maybe she was supposed to walk that deliberately towards the altar.

The man stood to wave the incense all around her many times as *Ammā* placed a dot of saffron on her forehead. She was guided to sit down behind the fruit, and *Ammā* crouched beside her, armed with her blood red termite hill of saffron. Neela put out her hands for more saffron to mark her wrists, her palms, the tops of her feet, and her forehead again. Meanwhile the man's lips moved in a rhythmic song I felt swept up in without knowing any of the words. Incense gradually clouded the air and in the middle of it all shone Neela, a yellow sun. Above the facade of her costume, her face appeared soulless. Her eyes were empty. She didn't blink when the red dust fell down upon her face from the layers of saffron across her forehead. The powder rested in clumps across the half-moons of her eyelashes. They must have become heavy, but still, she did not blink.

All the women in the room walked up onto the altar to hand her cards with money inside, boxes of jewelry, and packages wrapping new saris. We were already told of the gifts she would get, so when I saw them, I could predict what was inside. It was still exciting. This was the only time during the course of the entire evening that I wished it was me up there, receiving so much. Through it all, Neela maintained the look of a mannequin in a store window. Hours must have passed before it was finally finished and Neela was nearly covered in red powder. Some of the turmeric was placed on her hands and feet along with the saffron, but not as much of it. I thought of the hours it would take for her to wash it off later, and how long it would take *Ammā* and me to remove the flowers and undo her hair.

After the ceremony, Neela was placed like a doll on the floor near the front of the room so that people could photograph her. I wanted to help her up so we could run away into the darkness, but I had to stand in the background. I realised it was the first time that everyone was looking at someone, and it *wasn't* me. I was invisible to the crowds of Indians surrounding us. It suddenly didn't matter that I was a deaf-mute foreigner with freckled skin. For the first time, I felt like one of them.

NECESSARY RITUALS

When the ceremonial activities ended, everyone filed downstairs for a great feast. A hundred banana leaves lined the long tables. I couldn't sit next to Neela, but I was able to sit close enough to watch her. She ate the rice and selection of vegetarian sauces rhythmically and emotionlessly. I ate ravenously but flushed with embarrassment when I caught Neela watching me. She laughed for the first time that day. When people finished eating, the waiters came around with jugs of water to pour over our hands to wash off the food. Everyone folded their banana leaves and began to leave. It all ended so abruptly that before I knew it, it was just *Ammā*, Mathi, Neela, and I. We carried Neela's presents back to our house where she was able to remove her costume and wash off the red and orange powders.

Neela spent the next few months experimenting with different saris. Every day she was more beautiful. She moved along with the moon through her monthly cycles. Just before her bleeding, I tried to avoid asking her for help with school or anything. One day I said, *Where did you find that s-a-r-i?*

She burst into tears while signing, *I know it looks cheap, doesn't it?*

Her signing was becoming clearer. I was glad for that and I could handle her emotional outbursts, but there were times when she did things I hated. When we were with the other girls at school or in the village and they laughed at something, I would tap Neela's arm frantically and ask, *What's so funny?*

Neela, perfect Neela, would reply, *Nothing. You don't need to know, it's not important.*

I didn't feel equal to her. They were having fun, they were laughing at something stupid perhaps, but I was missing it. Granted, I missed nearly everything spoken around me, but it was different when I had a way to know. Neela could have told me, and she didn't.

၈

I loved Neela most when she was telling me stories. She started doing that when she mastered enough sign to create the three-dimensional pictures in the air necessary for storytelling. I enjoyed our visits to the temple more and more because she told me the stories of the Hindu gods whenever we went there.

We would walk to the temple in the early morning light. Most of the village was already awake. We could smell the poori and idli being cooked as our legs moved us past the houses of various sizes and shapes. Some were small and looked as if they were molded out of the dirt itself. They had thatch-roofs like the cottages in Ireland, only these roofs were made of palm leaves. Other houses were like ours, one floor and an outdoor staircase leading up to the roof.

In Ireland, we never ventured out onto a rooftop. There was too much wind and rain. Most Irish homes didn't have roofs with railings and flat spaces to sleep under the stars. The rooftops in this village were warm, inviting rooms opened to sky and dreams. They were in-between places: between earth and the heavens, places for watching a day's transition, the sun rising or setting. On a rooftop, time seemed to halt around me, separating me from the life down below and the shimmering lights above. As we walked to the temple, I eyed the empty rooftops of my village, wondering why nobody else felt their magic.

The temple was a square of deep grey stone walls surrounding what looked like a granite palace of layers and heights. It wasn't white like the temple near the astrologer in the mountains. Other temples had gold-plated roofs. Our temple's roofs were stone like its walls. It felt cave-like, which made it more exciting to me than the elaborate temples of other cities.

We had to leave our sandals by the Ganesh statue at the entrance. There was a pond next to the temple where we washed our feet before walking through the gates. It purified us. We lowered ourselves to the ground at the gates, some people rested their foreheads against the dirt, but *Ammā* didn't let us do that. Her fear of germs prompted her to claim it wasn't needed, that the respect itself was what was most important. I tried to remember, but sometimes my head accidentally touched the ground and Neela had to brush the dirt out of my hair before *Ammā* saw.

Inside the courtyard, we walked clockwise around the temple. In various places along the outer walls, there were statues of different gods. Each statue had its own pile of deep red saffron powder and some yellow and orange powders as well. The yellow was turmeric, but I wasn't sure what the orange was—maybe a mix of saffron and turmeric. Sometimes there was white, which I knew as Shiva's powder. Men wore the white on their foreheads and sometimes the red, while women wore the red and sometimes the white.

Neela told me stories of the gods in sign while we stood at each statue. It reminded me of school in Ireland when we read stories from the Bible, but the Bible never made me feel overcome with awe. The Bible didn't have such colours. And I never liked how bad the snake was supposed to be. I thought all animals were good, and Hinduism seemed to agree. One Hindu god was even a monkey. The animals were close to us here. They were respected. I looked into the eyes of the stray cats that roamed the temple, and they didn't seem small to me. They felt like huge creatures who knew more than I did.

Once we made it back to the temple's entrance, we could walk into the temple itself. It was always dark. We imagined there were creatures and spirits in the shadows. *Ammā* didn't let Neela sign to me in there because nobody was supposed to speak at all, even with hands. We lined up on the left, and a man came out of a doorway in the wall and placed the red and white powders before us in little silver dishes he cupped delicately with both hands. I copied Neela and placed my left middle finger into the bowls, one by one, and gave myself the red dot and white line on my forehead. I felt safe once that happened, as if the monsters around us could never harm me as long as I had those marks on my face.

We moved around the inner temple clockwise, too. Sometimes we brought offerings for certain statues, but I hadn't learned about all of the gods enough to know what to bring or what to ask for. Only Lakshmi. I asked her about me. I asked her why she was given to me, or why I was hers. Sometimes I asked her to take me back—to Ireland, to the sea.

She never answered.

One morning, as we walked back from the temple, Neela and I saw a tiny golden puppy limping across the street, dodging a wagon of hay pulled by large cows. We ran to help him, much to *Ammā's* distaste. She hated and feared dogs like most Indians. The dogs were trapped in their roles of street gangs, thieves, and bastard animals who barked or growled when people came too close. It wasn't their fault, though. Indians threw stones at them, never let them into their homes, and ran from them when they approached. I knew that if the Indians treated the dogs the way most people did in Ireland, the dogs would wag their tails and roam the streets healthy and happy. Instead, they were starved or beaten, their tails stuck between their legs as if they had been glued there.

It took me months to persuade Neela that the dogs weren't something to fear, and so by the time we saw a stray puppy in need, she was thoroughly convinced enough to pick him up and lavish him with caresses and murmurings. The puppy was overjoyed the way dogs often became when we gave them such unexpected love. She had to quickly put it back on the ground before *Ammā* started screaming. We turned to *Ammā,* each of us put our hands together as if in prayer and wagged our heads side-to-side, while Neela begged her to allow us to bring the puppy home.

Ammā waged a lifelong battle against dust and bacteria. According to her, diseases and sickness were everywhere. They lived in the dust that rose up from the ground in the heat and we had to do everything we could to keep them off our skin. When I thought of *Ammā*, I couldn't picture her without a broom or a cleaning rag in her hand. Sometimes, in my dreams, *Ammā* chased me with a cleaning sponge. She wanted to wipe my skin of every freckle I had because she was certain that they were dirt. I would wake, arms flailing, as I tried to push the sponge away. Neela laughed when I had those dreams.

She told me later what she had said that won over *Ammā:* "We will raise him, and feed him, and care for him all by ourselves! You won't need to touch him! We will keep him in the hut or outside, never in our house. And when he is healthy and grown he will protect us at night because we have no man to do that. Please, *Ammā,* please!"

We were elated to take turns carrying the small dirty puppy home with us. We named him Ariyan, because it was one of Shiva's thousand names. We thought it would help him become strong and grow into a great dog. A guard like Ganesh.

I was holding him when *Ammā* ordered us inside to help her begin cooking lunch. She scowled at me, although her striking Indian face was so similar to Neela's that even a scowl made me smile inside. I dutifully put Ariyan down when I reached the doorway of the house.

Not long after we adopted Ariyan, while I was going to the toilet at school, I found my left hand red with blood. It scared me even though I remembered what it was after a few minutes. I noticed that a few smears of blood had dried on my inner thighs and the inside of my sari skirt. I knew *Ammā* would want it all washed off immediately, but I was too humiliated to tell her.

I was scared of the hut in our backyard. How could I spend days inside that small space alone with the cockroaches and the ants? I felt alone enough without hearing the words around me, but at least I could observe whole scenes unfolding. I thought of the sunrises and sunsets that Neela and I watched from our rooftop. How could I miss them for days on end? When days could easily feel like months. The hut loomed before me.

I washed off my hand and the insides of my legs, and I rushed to find Neela. She would understand my fear and help me to hide it from *Ammā*. She didn't. Neela rushed us both home, and I was sent to the hut. At least, I was able to keep Ariyan with me at night.

I imagined I was in a torturous prison. I couldn't bear to do schoolwork. Instead, I wrote stories of ghosts and gods. I made up my own gods— Hinanuala, a warrior like Durga and Kali. Like most Hindu gods, she was always blue-skinned. She was Ganesh's lover because *Ammā* told us he had no lover. She fought sea monsters so that Lakshmi could be born in the milk of the waves and given over to Vishnu. Hinanuala was killed in battle and turned into a ghost. She still had indigo eyes like me, and she carried a torch so that women would always have light in the darkness. I used my coloured pencils to draw her like the posters of the Hindu gods we had taped to our walls. I drew her standing on a giant lotus, rising out of the sea, its trunks of green like sea serpents around her, coiling.

Finally, my bleeding stopped and *Ammā* let me out of the hut. I took my writings and drawings, folded them up, and hid them in my school books. I knew they were not good enough for Neela to see. It was awkward to see Neela again, though she embraced me and quickly asked, *Are you ok now?*

Yes, I replied.

After so long by myself, I was short of words, but Neela understood. She had been through it. I could read her eyes as I read Ariyan's and see the comprehension inside them, and we smiled. Though I was happy to be back with Neela, I missed Ariyan's small bony body beside mine at night. I could caress him and hold him as I had never done with Neela.

I also had to face the puberty ceremony. I tried to keep it out of my mind as Neela helped me put on my new saris, as we went shopping with *Ammā* in Pondicherry, and as we continued to wander off into the woods and the canyons whenever we could get away from *Ammā's* hawk-like eyes.

ॐ

On the morning of my ceremony, I sat on our back steps, looking at my Indian name—*Lakshmi*, written in blue across the middle of the card. The Tamil letters that formed my name were familiar enough to me that I could read them without thinking. The puberty card rested carefully in my hands freshly painted with henna. I tried to think of the food I would get to eat. That watered my mouth and relaxed my nerves. I could feel *Ammā* rushing around in the house below me. I knew she was ordering Neela and Mathi around, and I felt sorry for them, but not long ago Neela had also sat alone waiting for the henna to harden and crack against the skin of her hands, pinching as it pulled at tiny hairs here and there. Waiting to peel it off like a second layer of skin.

Later on, I was humiliated at my reflection in the mirror while *Ammā* and Neela dressed me in a bright yellow sari with gold stitching all along its edges. It made my skin look even lighter and the freckles stand out as if they really were patches of dirt. The henna spread out in bright red orange swirling lines across my hands and feet in designs Neela or I could never have hoped to create.

Ammā was running my ceremony exactly as she had done Neela's. Perhaps I should have been touched by the affection it implied but all I could think about were the crowds of people and the strange man in the white lungi who would initiate me into my womanhood. It felt like he was initiating me into Indian culture, rather than on a path all my own. If I went through this, would I ever leave this country or these people? I wondered what Father would have thought. I thought of sending him the puberty ceremony card, and then realised that he would never understand the Tamil. Still, it wasn't something I wanted him to know. Another secret to hide beneath the layers of fabric that swirled around my altered body.

They didn't know what to do because I was deaf. The words were important, but because I didn't know the local sign language and interpreters were pretty much unheard of in the village, we were left with Neela to act as my interpreter. I was dazed by the dark eyes watching and the smoke of the incense as it moved around my body, and the turmeric and saffron powders that were placed on my forehead over and over until I watched everything from behind eyelashes dusted with yellow and red. I worried that my sari would get stained by so much red powder, but *Ammā*, for the second time in her life perhaps, didn't care. It was holy powder. I suppose it couldn't carry diseases.

I focused my attention on random objects around me: the large bananas and mangoes on the fruit tray. The deep red powder on *Ammā's* finger tips. Neela's hands, though I didn't see their words. She fingerspelled a lot, and I watched her long fingers moving from one letter into another. They had henna painted on them, too, but not as much or as intricate as mine. I watched the face of the man in the white lungi. The transparency of his crystal beads. People mounted the stage and handed me envelopes, packages of assorted sizes, and shook my hands with mouths moving incessantly. I watched as Neela struggled to interpret. I felt guilty that I still couldn't focus on the words. Her arms and hands moved fluidly like a dancer. I knew when she was guessing at signs or improvising, or when she got caught behind the pace of the speech. The actual words fell to the ground because they didn't matter to me at all.

Eventually I was led off the stage and made to sit on the side of the entrance to the room for photographs. I must have looked like a crazed sadhu with my face covered in powder. I tried to smile, as most Western people did in photos, but I found I had already become Indian, because the corners of my mouth wouldn't move up or down. My face was frozen in the classic blank stare most Indians gave for photographs.

Downstairs, I mechanically inserted the rice and sauces into my mouth. I watched Neela, and I knew her hands must be tired. She had never signed for so long, even when she told me intricate stories. I pitied her. I wanted to rub her back, as Mother used to do for me when I was sick. Could I touch her like that?

ANTS

One night we had finished dinner and washed ourselves with buckets of cold water. During the smoldering time of year just before the monsoon, we took bucket baths at least twice a day. A few months after I turned thirteen, the heat crawled into my bug bites on my right arm and burst out of them as yellow pus. We tried an old herbal remedy of layering hot turmeric paste onto my blisters overnight, and I went to sleep with my arm out to the side so it wouldn't be disturbed.

I woke to a strange sensation on my arm. When I opened my eyes, I saw tiny armies of ants eating away at my pus. They were the same reddish brown colour as the dirt outside. They crawled in single file wavering lines across the black tiles on the floor like an orderly procession of particles of dust. My body froze. Neela woke and when she saw the ants, she began to scream. *Ammā* promptly shuffled into the room with questioning eyes. When she saw the ants, she screamed, too, but then she dragged me outside and wiped them off me. I was relieved. All I wanted to do was to get them off, but I couldn't move by myself. Once all of the ants were gone, I hugged *Ammā* for the first time. She took the physical affection awkwardly. I missed Mother then because *Ammā* had acted like a mother, but the lack of touch and easy communication between us was a continuous reminder that she was not Mother.

During the day it was hard not to keep moving. I was afraid if I stood still for too long the ants would come back. I looked at the spots on my arms and feared I was becoming like the ants myself. Oxygen entered their bodies through millions of holes, entered, transformed, and left through the same holes as carbon dioxide. Would I breathe through the pus-filled scabs if I could not make them close? If I could not heal, would I transform?

When the day was over, we were left alone in our room with the crimson and black tile floors. We lay in our saris staring up at the glowing yellow light hanging from the ceiling. Neela was waiting for me to tell her which story I wanted her to draw in the air before bed. I was busy watching the geckos. They were almost the same shade of dirty cream as the ceiling and the walls, so I had to look closely. One was chasing a fly, and the other was snapping at him. They dashed across the room faster than our tired eyes could ever follow. A giant spider was crawling up the side of the wall near the red door. The paint peeled beneath her long furry legs. Sea green crumbled off the walls so that the flecks of it gathered together all along the edges of the room. We swept the floors daily, but the chips of paint, ruptured by tiny animal legs, always fell.

Everything used to feel so dirty to me here, but as I watched the life moving in our room, I felt happier for it. I turned to look at Neela's face. Her skin was dark brown like most south Indian women. Changing in shade from one part of her body to another. Her hands were the colour of coffee beans, while her face and neck were a few shades darker than chai. Her thick eyelashes were black like her hair. I loved the wideness of her mouth, her lips curved like the petals of a lotus. My eyes wandered down to the faded red string around her neck that held the small silver disc with a tiny Ganesh figure etched onto its smooth surface. I had the same necklace. Neela noticed my eyes and smiled while spelling out G-a-n-e-s-h and nodding her head in that side-to-side way. I let my head move likewise as I watched her gather the folds of her blue sari and stand up in the centre of our mattress. I edged my body up against the back wall of the room so that she had enough space to draw.

Ganesh was my favourite story because he had an elephant's head the same colour as a seal. He was her favourite story because she thought how funny it would be to have an animal's head on a human body. Even the geckos and the spider seemed to freeze while her arms and fingers traced pictures in the air.

She drew Parvati, the mother, at home waiting for her husband, Shiva, to return. The air shimmered in dynamic shades of pink and gold. Perfect Indian woman face with gold nose ring. Exactly round red bindi on her forehead. Parvati was laughing. Parvati created a full-grown son, Ganesh, out of turmeric so that he could watch the house while Shiva was gone. Ganesh stood at the door so Parvati could feel safe.

Shiva's ominous form was suddenly outlined in the doorway of our bedroom. As if he had just now entered from the wild dark outside. His skin was blue like Neela's dress. Three white slashes of powder across his forehead. He was outraged to find a strange young man protecting the house. In his anger, Shiva grasped a gold sword and chopped off Ganesh's head without asking Parvati anything!

I watched her form rise from her seat in thematic slow motion and scream as Neela drew the head rolling to the side of the room and I could imagine hearing the sound of the *thud* it made against the wall. Parvati burst into tears and told Shiva he had just cut off the head of her new son! Shiva was so upset he ordered his guards to go out and take the head of the first animal they could find. Their figures were drawn smaller and smaller as they rushed away into the forests beyond our window.

The elephant was so large! Neela couldn't draw the whole of it. We laughed, like always, at her failed attempts. His head, however, fit the gallant son perfectly and everyone was happy. Ganesh became a god of good luck and protection. Elephants were also wise and loyal. When she finished her drawing, we knew he stayed in our room and protected us from the demons in the dark outside.

Neela was tired when she finished that night's story. She had been busy following me around during the day as I ran from the ants. We sat half-off the edge of the bed to do the ritual *Ammā* had taught us for my blisters. Neela liked to hold the spoon as I mixed the turmeric powder and water to form a paste. She held the spoon over a candle to heat it. I tried not to flinch when she dabbed the hot paste onto my arm. Soon all my blisters were covered in small yellow globs that felt better than any Western medicine I had tried before. We sat for a few minutes so that the paste could dry up in the air blown by the small fan. We turned the light off and kept the candle burning.

After we lay down to sleep, me on the side near the floor so that my arm could stretch out, Neela felt afraid for me. The candle was low but I could see her slender form leaning over me from time to time to check for ants. I wanted to touch that shadow of her body above me in the dim of the tiny fire at our side. This new feeling made my skin tingle. My heart began to beat faster. Was there something wrong with me? I just wanted to bury my face in the soft curtain of her dark hair.

My left hand reached up involuntarily. It found a home against her cheek that curved into it when she smiled. She leaned into me like a shadow returning to its body after a long absence. Her face snuggled mine as her hair fell around us and I couldn't see anymore. I didn't need to see or hear anything else. I felt my own forehead squeeze together as my eyebrows lifted and tears rimmed my eyes, leaning over my lashes like children trying to see over the edge of something, children about to leap into the unknown, the yearned for, the future about to change in a moment.

Our bodies felt charged like lightning and the monsoon rain was about to pour down through our eyes. One kiss released the floods. I was thirteen and it was my first taste of lips upon lips. The first touch to surpass the closeness of Mother's. Neela's body gave off heat that Mother only had inside. She touched me in ways Mother never did—opening me like a shell. Our saris were loosened around us like two blue seas, hers the colour of the depths and mine the lighter almost-green colour of the surface, with yellow and peach fragments of a sunset splashed across it. The dwindling light of the candle in the corner of my eye was the sun of my childhood setting beside us: my sisterly feeling towards Neela flickering away.

We unbuttoned our sari tops slowly, floating between fabric and darkness. We didn't know we could be so happy in the belly of our fears. And the demons outside didn't interrupt our joy in each other. I lowered my head beneath her to kiss the breasts that had barely begun to grow. She laughed. I could feel her chest trembling and placed my left hand over her mouth and cheek to feel their smile and the quick bursts of air coming through. I laughed, too. I didn't realise I made any sound until her soft hand was over my mouth.

Sorry, you were being loud. I watched her shadow say.

It's ok, I understand. Inside the shame spread.

Good. I hate to change you. Had she?

It's better than people hearing and catching us. An obvious reply. What I meant was *please don't stop.*

What are we doing? She looked insecure for the first time that night. I wanted to console her, to bring her back to me.

I don't know, but it feels nice. You're beautiful. I attempted.

No, you're beautiful. Her eyes were so wide that I believed them.

Laughter again. This time we both covered our mouths with each other's hands. Hands over hands over mouths. We didn't touch below the small of our bellies. Fears and secrets were hiding beneath my skirt that I couldn't yet uncover. Even to myself. The night passed slowly. In our half-sleep, half-dreams, we couldn't stop our fingers from moving across each other. The candle lasted until dawn. One sun passing light to another.

The sun rose quickly that morning. As soon as she could see well enough, Neela grabbed at my arm where the crusty turmeric dots had hardened and cracked. Some had fallen off like the paint peeling off our walls. I couldn't resist her careful examination, but I was too tired to be as excited about the results. She signed in such a jumble that my eyes couldn't hope to follow, so I looked down and saw the reason right away. The ants had left me alone.

DARKNESS

I was fourteen when the darkness started. It was a year after the night my arms became splattered with blisters from the ants. The night when Neela first touched me and I could feel my entire body singing to her, wanting to sign, move, speak.

Finally, it said.

Neela and I sneaked away together often. Our bedroom became our own private temple in homage to our favourite stories and each other's bodies. We kept a picture of Lakshmi besides our picture of Ganesh on the wall. We conversed in sign and wrote in Tamil. Sometimes we just stared and let the words flow back and forth beneath our eyelids.

Neela's skin was almost black, like many South Indians. She had a round face and thin eyebrows. Her hair flowed down to her waist in soft waves. Her eyes were dark, but when the sunlight shone in them, I was able to see tiny flecks of gold around her pupils. We liked to compare our lips in the mirror because they were so different from each other. My lips were narrow and pointy. Pale against paler skin. Neela's lips didn't have the same two points on top that mine did. Hers were rounded and full. The kind of lips you can't stop thinking about kissing. The kind of lips you want to feel on your skin. I was self-conscious of my freckles, but Neela said they were beautiful. She licked them sometimes.

Father hadn't written in months. He was somewhere in Indonesia. I pictured him diving with sharks, examining the corals shining with shades of red, orange, and yellow, rivaling the brightness of the saris around me.

The day the darkness began was a day like any other. It was a sweltering afternoon. Neela and I went home from school early. We wanted to do something bad. Our newfound womanhood leaned us towards experimentation. The canyons called to us—promises of daytime nudity, swimming in our favourite pool, making love in the sunlight. I was thinking of the curve of Neela's wet hip against the canyon rocks as she pulled her body up onto the ledge. The way I would try to brush the red dirt flecks off her skin, but they would only stick to my fingers until we jumped back into the water. The way her dark hands tangled in the auburn waves of my hair as she braided wet flowers into it.

I didn't notice Neela's *Ammā* standing near the shops as we passed. Her eyes met Neela's, and I could feel the ground shaking below us. She was furious to see us so far from school and *why*?! I read the Tamil on her lips without needing anything written down. Normally that would have made me feel proud, but I was terrified.

Neela pretended to cry, and *Ammā* said something terrible to her. I didn't know what it was. I pinched Neela's arm on our way back to school repeatedly, but she would not tell me.

After school, we were sent to our room without dinner. On our shared bed on the floor, Neela finally signed, *A demon will come here tonight.*

I laughed. I brought her under our blue elephant sheets, and told her we were safe there. *Remember G-a-n-e-s-h? He will protect us!*

She shook her head. *Not now.*

How can I do anything if I don't know what's going on?

She sat for a moment. Tears made salt rivers upon her face, prominent against the dark of her skin. Her eyes were full of fear. She never showed fear without courage lurking behind it. Her ego was strong like a snake— but it wasn't strong now. She began slowly.

I'm going to write the name down, then you burn paper and I'll tell the story. Ok?

NĪLĪ, she wrote.

I burned the paper and waited. My stomach grumbled. My eyes were tired, although the sky was still violet. We both sat cross-legged beneath the blue sheet. The grey and white batik elephants froze in their procession to watch the story told by the moving hands below.

Her story went like this:

In a small hut by the river, there lived a man and his wife. She was by far the most beautiful woman of the entire village and the man felt lucky to have her. She became pregnant and throughout the pregnancy, she was very sick. They were both afraid for the child, but the woman was strong. She held on through her contractions until she was finally able to squeeze the baby out of her. Once the little boy was in her husband's arms, she died.

The father wept as he washed his healthy son and cut the cord linking him to his mother.

The ghost of the man's dead wife materialised out of the far shadow in the corner. The man was overjoyed to see his wife's soul come to bless her baby and kiss him goodbye. But as she glided closer, he saw a deep blackness in her eyes. The man bolted out of his home and ran with his child, still damp in his arms, up to the hut of a saint. He felt her breath upon the back of his neck. She whispered into his ears, "Let me kill the child."

The baby wailed.

When they reached the hut, the door was already open for him. Saints knew such things before they happened. As the man entered, the door slammed behind him. Strange herbs were hanging on small strings from the ceiling of the hut. The saint sat cross-legged by a glowing fire. He wore only a white lungi and clear crystal beads hanging from his neck. His hair was long and tied back with a string. His eyebrows were thick. His deep brown eyes radiated peace.

The saint spoke in a whisper. "Your wife's sorrow at her own death and separation from her child has caused her to become a demon. She will try to kill you and the child until she has succeeded." He took a gleaming silver blade from beneath his skirt and handed it to the man. "This knife will protect you both from her as long as you hold it. Lose it, and you will not escape your death again."

The man understood. He replied over and over, "*Nandre nandre nandre.*"

He crept back out into the dark.

His wife was waiting, but when she saw the knife she vanished into the night. With the knife in his hands, he walked back home and slept until dawn. As the sun rose, the light comforted him. He began to prepare his wife's body for burial. First, however, he had to carry the child down to the river for a bath and gather water for washing the body. As the husband made his way to the river, the demon took on solid form in the sunlight and went before the leader of their village. She cried before him: "My husband has gone mad and stolen my child and he has a knife he will use to kill me with if I get near them! Please help me!"

The village leader responded: "Where is your husband, so that I may demand his knife from him and give you back your child?"

"The river, the river." She moaned and followed him with an invisible smile upon her perfect lips.

When the leader saw the husband with the blade in his hands, he yelled: "Set down your knife and give your child to his mother! You must not abuse her like this!"

The husband cried: "You don't understand! My wife is dead! That woman behind you is a demon!"

"I will hear nothing of that! She has been weeping and weeping over your madness! Drop that knife! End this now!"

The man looked to the heavens. He looked towards the saint's hut at the top of the hill. Neither the saint nor the god Shiva seemed to be near enough to help him. Giving in to his fate, he kissed his child, and replied: "Let it be finished then!"

The man let his sacred knife slide through his hands as the demon flew towards him. She grabbed her child and ate him. As the remaining chunks of his tiny body fell from her hands and his blood poured into the river, she seized her husband with her long nails and tore into his flesh, too. And she disappeared.

The story was terrifying, but I didn't know how it related to what *Ammā* had told her. Seeing the question in my eyes, she signed, *Wait, I'll finish.*

I waited as she rested her hands on her skirt. I let my own hands press against her knees for comfort and found that she was still shaking. She continued. *Mothers here tell this story to their children. If we pretend to cry, they say we are N-ī-l-ī crying and once the sun goes down, she will come and get us.*

My hands couldn't move to reply. We clasped against each other in the terror Neela had shared. Between us, the terror grew so large it filled the room. There were moments when we felt Nīlī's hands scratching at our sheet that we kept covering our heads—a mystical barrier. We didn't notice the sweat dripping down the sides of our faces, down our necks, between our breasts. We didn't lie down for the fear that she would crush us beneath her. The night passed from one gasp to another.

After the story of Nīlī, I tried to think of my own mother, remembering her arms around me and how safe and magical I felt to be part of a legend like her. I was a part of the sea and the most peaceful animal to swim its waters. We were seal people, not demons. I touched the webs between my fingers lovingly, imagining Mother's hands in my own. I thought memories of Mother would eradicate my fears, but I couldn't rid my mind of the image of Nīlī eating her own child. When we went to the canyon weeks later, I thought the redness of the water had come from the blood of Nīlī's baby.

It was only dirt. There was not much to fear in the daylight. The sun shone far into corners. Children laughed and ran in the streets with the animals. Even the jungle-like woods of palms and eucalyptus trees were familiar enough.

Being deaf in the dark was something else altogether. Neela told me about the sounds in the dark: footsteps. Creaking. Branches shaking and snapping against each other with the wind. Animals howling, rushing, whining, barking. The footsteps are the most important. They matter when you are alone. Hearing footsteps can save you. You know when to hide or rush home. You know what directions to avoid.

I couldn't hear footsteps. Everything in the dark reaches me through my eyes and my skin. I see shadows, glimpses, movements. Most of my surroundings don't exist unless they are something I can touch, see, or smell. But I do feel things. Every motion in the dark has a domino effect.

I had to learn this slowly. Birds fly away when something large approaches. The smell of the wind changes. Out of the corners of my eyes I see wispy ghost-like tatters of moving air. I had to learn to get used to it. I used to think it was fairies. Or spirits. In the dark, I learned to live in my belly, follow its sensations. Run or hide when it told me to. I had to give it reins, give it ropes to lead me.

Ireland: the landscape of my childhood is nearly vacant. Darkness spreads over the cliffs, hills, and fields fringed by rough seas. I walk through it as if I have eyes that can see the daylight greens, greys, blues. Regardless of colours or visions, my feet catch on rocks, slip through mud-filled pockets of plant-filled earth. Thorns and the scent of rotting blackberries. The lack of predatory animals means my greatest enemies come from the land itself—bushes that draw blood, fences topped with barbed wires, unseen pockets of space beyond cliffs ending in rough seas able to swallow young girls in a single gasp.

I find my way through these things without ears or eyes in the darkness, and it becomes second nature. I let my feet carry me up the hills so I can look upon the vast ocean at my door. Torches are objects fit for smashing. The landscape is an animal, and I crawl up its backbone in the dark. I am proud.

ॐ

India: I walk into the woods down the path behind our house. The land is a playground for its creatures. Scorpions crawl out from the canyons. Cobras sleep in the bushes. Owlets dart from treetop to treetop. I see their wings in quick flashes of white, and they are gone. Stray dogs lurk with bared teeth for the hapless shadow that may pass into their territories. And worse—drunk village men looking for anything to push themselves into. All of them shrouded. All of them silent.

I walk into their arms, weak as a lamb. But here there is more to feel in the movements around me. Insects encircle me like sparks. Tiny pinches of vibrations flow through the woods. I work to learn their language. It is the same as learning the language of a smile or someone's eyes.

I needed the power I could only receive from the darkness of Indian woods. I went through a period of training. The story of Nīlī had inspired it. I began taking walks alone in the dark. Girls were not supposed to do this, but I had to be strong. I would learn to take comfort in blackness, prove that I didn't need ears, and I could do without eyes, too. I waged my own war against Fear, and I felt myself winning.

It was the first thing about me that Neela didn't understand. She tried to stop me, but I was partly rebelling against her. Neela had begun to change in her own way. She shed her youth like a skin, and in her growth, she became magnificent. Everyone was captivated by her, and I understood the way she swayed towards the attention. A dancing cobra in the long yellow grass. Even boys tried to talk to her. *Ammā* was fussing about marriage arrangements. It alarmed me that Neela didn't seem to mind. I wouldn't be able to keep her, a secret hidden in the folds of my skirt. She would leave me. I knew it in her eyes. She was turning from me more and more.

Around the time we were both turning fifteen, Neela started talking to boys and spending time in giggling groups of girls. Every now and then she forgot about me. I would stand there, unable to discern words from the mouths of her friends, and she wouldn't tell me. I was jealous of her rising popularity and angry with myself for the words I couldn't hear. I was naïve. I didn't know about the real shadows around us. The real demons. Until the night I saw the black spirits crawling over buildings like strange animals.

It was a Saturday night. Neela and I tiptoed out of the house. We met up with two boys from our school who had mopeds. I don't remember their names. I was uneasy riding on the back of the strange boy's bike, but Neela forced me into it. She was excited. She even gave the boy she was with her secret smile. That smile used to be mine. I wanted to reach out and peel it off her, and hold it inside my sari top, so that he couldn't ever see it again. But I kept my hands down at my sides. The boy with me brought paper and a pen. He wrote such messy Tamil, I could barely read it.

YOU LIKE MOPED? ARE YOU HAPPY TO RIDE WITH ME?

I looked at Neela. She was laughing and speaking in whispers. I could tell by the way her head leaned forward as the boy bent down to hear her. I looked back into the expectant eyes of the boy in front of me. I smiled. He couldn't tell my smile was empty.

We sat sideways on the back of their bikes. It was always fun to ride that way. The boys weren't used to having girls sitting on the back of their bikes, and the way we had to sit with our saris made it harder for them to balance, I smiled to myself and hoped the other boy would fall and Neela would land in the dirt, crying. Then I could help her. I could show her why boys were stupid and riding mopeds would never be more fun than what she and I could do alone in our bed.

As we started moving, however, I couldn't help but give in to an unwanted feeling of exhilaration. Perhaps it was the feeling of doing something forbidden—young women out in the night with boys. Riding mopeds down the highway towards the city of Pondy, our nickname for Pondicherry. I held onto the thin waist in front of me until I quickly felt confident enough to hold onto the back of his bike instead. The wind made me wish I had wings and could fly around all night like an owlet.

The palm trees along the road were tall, their large leaves were a beautiful shade of deep green filling the sky. Lights lit up random temples on the roadsides, hotels, tiny shack restaurants with plastic chairs and tables outside. I could smell the dosai being fried and the spice of the coconut and ground yellow pea sauce. Fried rice. Fried noodles. Fried eggs. I would get hungry for an instant, and we were gone.

We moved faster and faster towards the city.

As we entered Pondy, the roads were crowded with mopeds, bicycles, and cars. The tiny tea shops multiplied and the scents changed to cardamom and sugar. Sweet shops were on both sides filled with rows of different coloured confections, pastries, and squares of mysterious-looking desserts. I longed for the large silver pots of rose syrup with the floating milk balls in them called *gulab jamun*—my favourite sweets.

We hurried through the traffic to the cinema. It smelled of popcorn and fizzy drinks, similar to the cinemas in Ireland, but this one was much larger. It had plush red velvet seats, and the films were at least three hours long, so they had an intermission. I didn't always need to hear the films we watched. They were so dramatic. Everything could be read in the faces. They played half a dozen songs during the movie where everyone in the film would suddenly begin dancing and changing scenery and outfits. It was always entertaining.

This was the first time we were at the cinema at night. There were mostly men around us, which made us stand closer to each other. The boys became protectors for Neela and me. They kept us away from the drunken men and the men who stared too much. They stayed with us the entire time. Even during the film, the boys were respectful. My boy didn't even try to hold my hand. I was almost disappointed, but adults didn't touch very often in public either.

We left the theatre in a confusing mass of mopeds and motorcycles. We drove for a while before we stopped at a tea stand. The chai felt warm and sweet down my throat, and the boys brought us *gulab jamun*. Neela gave me a wink when they handed the tiny silver bowls to us, and I knew she had told them to get it for me. I was embarrassed. It tasted wonderful anyway.

The boys had to get us back in a hurry. We had been gone at least four hours. During the ride back, the boys drove side-by-side on the road so they could talk to each other. Neela was laughing at their conversation, until she looked at me in apology. She couldn't sign to me and hold onto the bike at the same time. I was embarrassed again and looked away.

It was there, as I rode on that boy's bike, that I first saw them: the black spirits. I watched the dimly lit villages as we passed. I felt invisible and I wanted to let go. I wanted to take my hands off the bike and let my body fall off the back to bounce like a doll against the blue cement below us. I almost did it involuntarily. The shadows stopped me.

Nearly imperceptible black shapes crawled over the rooftops of some of the buildings in one of the villages. I had to stare until I believed what I saw. At first it was blurry, something to be taken as darkness itself, and nothing more. Then the shadows reached and moved as if they were actually crawling over the edges of the roofs. It chilled me and I began to tremble. I was reminded of Nīlī. Was she there, too? Was she one of those black ghost-like creatures, barely human?

After a while, I closed my eyes and held tighter to my bike seat until my fingers cramped, and I did not let go until we reached our village. We quickly said goodbye, walked home, and slipped back into our room and our bed like shadows ourselves.

Neela began to peel off my sari as we lay under our sheet. She moved her fingers over my still-shaking skin and warmed me where I was cold. She breathed life back into me beneath our little elephants, and I forgave her all of it. The entire night became a distant memory when I was faced with her slim body pressed into mine like a clam in a shell. Fear sat in the doorway like a stray animal waiting to be fed, but it was the shadows' turn to disappear. My universe filled up once more with only Neela. I held her close until dawn.

MIRAGE

After I saw the black spirits crawling over the village buildings, I realised that they were crawling over me, too. Neela ruled me like a goddess on her lotus throne with four sets of arms holding me. I felt her in every shift of the waters around me. I forgot everyone else. But she was slowly forgetting me.

I was fluent enough in Tamil that I could read entire books without looking up any more words than the other students at my level who could speak fluently. The boys looked at me in admiration similar to the awe that Neela had inspired. Yet when they looked at her, even though they could never hope to touch her as I did each night, I was jealous. I worried that she would let one of those boys touch her, or worse, kiss the lips I claimed with all the passion I could gather and pour into her lungs. I dreamed that I was her reason. The air she breathed. Without me, she would shrivel up and die.

One afternoon we were in the canyons, my favourite place besides the sea. The red dirt hills on either side of us were our fortress. Scorpions, black butterflies, and goats high on the cliffs eating from the green surrounded us. Neela and I were making love against the red mud by the pool of water. She was above me, her fingers pushing in and sliding back out. Rhythmic. I was inside her, too. I loved the feeling of our breasts against each other. She had pushed me against the mud-lathered rocks a bit rougher than usual. In a flash I was back on the stone cliffs of Ireland and a man was—

No. I stopped the flashback before it could finish, but Neela immediately knew there was something wrong. She eased her fingers out of me and signed, *What's wrong? Are you ok?*

No, I'm sorry. The signs made me cry as I watched them move invisibly off my hands and into her mind.

I knew I had ruined things. I would have to tell her or risk a deeper rift between us than I already felt. I still wonder if I staged the entire thing as a last attempt to keep her. We pulled our wet saris back over us and lay on the rocks in the sunlight. Signing slowly with my eyes downcast, staring into the pool of water, I told her the story of my rape at twelve years old, how it still haunted me and I had never kissed or touched a boy. I couldn't because when I saw boys, I saw that man standing behind them like a shadow.

Neela's face transformed from soft to hard. As I had hoped, she wanted to fix me. She explained to me a way that the yogi masters controlled their own inner demons and their memories of bad things by traveling back to the moment and pulling out the demon. They would kill it in the present moment so that it did no more harm to the person. The memory would lose its power.

We rubbed mud over ourselves so that our skin was red like the goddess Kali. We called upon Kali for blood and power and protection. We sat cross-legged, knees to knees, hands in hands, face to face. We closed our eyes together and traveled back in time to the scene of my violation. Together we each grabbed an arm of the man and we dragged him back, or rather, forward, to our canyon. I had a stick prepared behind me. It was shaped like a scythe. I swung it through the air and slashed into the man's neck. Blood flowed out as he choked. Neela covered her ears while he screamed. I held the scythe in my hands, balanced in the air, for what seemed like ages. As we wondered what to do with the body, it disappeared. I turned to Neela questioningly.

K-a-l-i took it away! She signed with a smile I could not yet return.

Neela walked me back to the house with an air of dignity. As if she was proud of what she had helped me accomplish. I couldn't tell her what I really felt, so I let her bask in her own glory for another chance to hold her that night.

Mathi was growing faster than we were. He was a foot taller than me by then. He also began communicating more in sign. One afternoon he let me ride on the back of his motorcycle when he drove to Pondy to buy spices for *Ammā*. I was surprised at his consideration. Neela had been out with a group of girls, and I stayed behind. I did that when I couldn't handle their fast-paced conversation. I had lately been feeling more and more like I held Neela back, so it was easier for me to stay at home and play with our dog Ariyan.

Mathi wore Western pants and T-shirts most of the time now, like his classmates at the University down the road towards Pondy. He stayed at home like most students, especially those who lived as close to the school as we did. But he had to have his motorcycle. His skin was lighter than Neela's, and his eyes shined beneath their long dark lashes. He was almost pretty. I think he wanted to wear his hair long, but *Ammā* wouldn't allow it. However, he kept his hair stubbornly as long as he possibly could—so that the thick waves hung down nearly into his eyes and covered the tops of his ears. Sometimes I had to stop my hands from reaching up and touching it.

Mathi and I stopped at the beach on our way home from Pondy. The day was hot. Sweat crisscrossed my body in little rivers. His eyes looked into mine. I could almost get lost in their darkness, forget he was a boy, forget he was like a brother, forget he wasn't Neela. But I kept my distance, even when Neela went out at night with boys and without me. He was telling me about what he was learning in school. Laughing at his teachers. From what Mathi told me, I saw that the young people learned in an environment with less control and more freedom. Women could be smart in other ways beyond the home. Because I was from Ireland, Mathi felt that I understood it more than Neela or *Ammā* ever could.

I'm going to go places, see the world, see America. This place is old and not growing, not moving with the times. His hands moved with his yearning.

It was the first time he was sharing his feelings with me. I agreed with some of them, but I was happy here. I was often ignored or stared at during my days at school or when Neela and I were signing to each other in town. In Ireland, I was seen more as different rather than disabled. But in India I was a member of a lower caste due to my deafness. My whiteness and the fact that I was obviously far from the country of my birth confused people. I ignored them more easily than they were able to ignore me. I could just focus my eyes elsewhere and the faces around me blended into a world of sari colours. Neela shone like the sun before me. The way others treated me didn't matter when I was with her.

Study hard so you excel at the University and you can go. Yes, I thought, go. So that it would be just Neela and me. I liked Mathi, but as I sat on that beach, I wished for him to transform into his sister or disappear.

You don't understand anything about Tamil culture, do you? I'm supposed to stay here and take care of my mother. If I make any money, I have to give it to her.

I know that. I have seen it here, but I don't know what to tell you.

A tiny glimmer flashed in his eyes as he looked into mine particularly intensely. *Stay here and marry me. You can be near Neela forever.*

He *knew.* I always thought maybe he would detect something between

Neela and me, or catch us one night, but I assumed he would shout it out as soon as he noticed it. I didn't figure him for hiding something that was utterly forbidden. I didn't understand why I loved Neela, and she didn't understand why she loved me. We imagined that the people around us would kill us if they found out. But we couldn't help how we felt. We couldn't change it and we couldn't suppress it. It simply was. I dug my feet into the sand and looked away. He must have thought that marrying me would be his passport to other places. I didn't have to go with him. I could always stay with Neela. He tapped my arm, which made me cringe slightly from the pretty eyes, the handsome face. When I looked up at him, he signed, *Mother loves you, too.*

I stood up. Looked down into his face and signed firmly, *No.* I ran. I didn't look back until I was in the village, surrounded by people and shops. He wasn't there.

Neela wasn't home when I arrived. Ariyan was frantic with excitement, but I couldn't stop and play with him. I wanted to tell her about Mathi. I decided to walk to the canyons. She probably went to Pondy with some girls, so it would be some time before she came back. Ariyan followed me, his mouth flashing open in small barks whenever we passed other dogs. I hoped they wouldn't fight. Usually I didn't let Ariyan accompany me to the canyons, but I was lonely.

Empty paths of red dirt and tiny insects passed under my feet. The long greenish blue leaves of the eucalyptus swayed above me. I kept adjusting my sari as I moved, even though it wasn't falling out of place. We passed other neighbourhood dogs more peacefully than I expected. It must have been the heat of the day weighing on even the animals. They were sleeping in the shadows of the banyan trees in the distance. Soon I was away from the houses and the village. I felt better once I was alone. The path widened as the cliffs of the canyon slowly rose on either side of me. Ariyan played with the butterflies, leaping and chasing, but their black little wings carried them away too swift for him to follow.

I neared the pond where Neela and I liked to swim after many minutes of dazed walking. When I came close, I could see disturbance in the water. I was about to turn away, but something pushed me forward, silent as the butterflies in the wind. A single butterfly froze in mid-flight—a black silhouette against the hazy whitish blue sky. A lock of hair hung down over my left eye, its tired wave rested against the folds of sari across my chest. Me, the invisible girl, crept up to the edge of the pool and followed the ripples of the water across it. They rhythmically hit against two naked forms at the far end. The same place where Neela—

I forgot to be invisible as I stared into the eyes of a girl with long black hair flowing into the water like pools of dark blood around her. The wide back of a boy with short dark hair moved towards her gently, rocking. The girl's hand came up to her mouth, covering the soft, full lips I knew by heart. I backed up against a rock. All the air in my body left through my opened mouth. I coughed. Her hand dropped down, spread out flat, and made a shaking circle on the back of the faceless boy.

Sorry, the hand said.

Sorry? I thought. Sorry she was fucking him, or sorry I caught her? Sorry she was betraying me in the very place where she and I always—

I stumbled back to escape the vision my eyes kept telling me was wrong.

Mirage. Illusion. Dream. Ghosts.

The canyon walls were closing in around me. I would be the first white girl to die by suffocation of pounds and pounds of red dirt in South India. I lifted my sari skirts and ran towards the only other place for me—the sea.

THE SEA

I wanted to swim to Ireland, swim to Father in his ship somewhere southeast. I wanted to find Mother beneath the surface of the water and be able to breathe there, too. I untied my hair and tightened my sari around my hips, tucking it in as far as I could. I knew the waves would thrash me. I had to get beyond their breaking point to the stretch of calm between my body and the sky. I felt stares from the Indian men in their hyena packs on either side of me, but I ignored them. I barely paused to place my sandals in the sand. I lifted my sari skirt as far as I dared as my legs danced over the ridges of waves. When the water felt too rough for me to stand or move without being knocked over, I dove into it.

As my body cut its way into the sea, a change slowly passed under my skin. The webs between my fingers and toes stretched and I could pull and kick my way deeper towards the quiet sand below. My anger fueled me and I climbed my way into the sea, into myself. I wanted to be a crab within a shell. I wanted to squeeze my body into a shape other than mine. Water felt better than the air around me. It cooled the fire inside. Soft jellied bodies touched my cheeks as I moved. Tiny fish poked my bare legs. I dug my webbed hands into the cold sand beneath me and kept climbing. I didn't panic until my hands were touching the sharp, uneven surfaces of coral and undersea rocks. I opened my eyes to the watery darkness and found I could see clearer than when I was above water. I could see the ground stretching out, mountainous with a deep blue sky that faded to light blue far above.

I looked up at the surface of the sea moving gently. I could not see where the sand reached the shore, nor could I feel the crashing vibration of distant waves. I was also—breathing? I brought my hand up to my mouth. No—I wasn't breathing. But I didn't need air. Large shapes glided over the mountains ahead of me. Tails wagged and bodies swayed. I was clinging to a large coral-crusted rock, watching schools of fish darting away as I kicked my feet, trying to remain balanced.

A few moments later my lungs seemed to remember their humanity, and I felt the pressure of the underwater world squeezing me. I kicked off the rock and sent my body upwards. I swam with every bit of energy I had left. My sari began to unravel and catch on the rocks. It hung down like a preposterous tail or sea serpent. I didn't want to be any sort of snake, but I couldn't let it go. I grasped the other end before the entire thing decided it would rather live underwater. With a scream, I surfaced. The air warmed me after the chill of the deep sea, but I had to continuously kick my tired legs while clutching my sari in my arms and searching for the beach along the horizon. Water kept sliding over my eyes and everything blurred. In one direction, I could see the dying flames of the sun casting a halo of orange and red over a long row of black palm tree silhouettes.

The rest of the sky was darkening into shades of violet and I was scared of the large moving shapes I saw below. If the sea was really my home, I wasn't used to it. I wasn't as equipped as Mother, and I doubted I could survive the night. Already exhausted, I didn't swim nearly as far as most sea creatures did in a day. I had to get back. Survival took over my limbs and my lungs, even though my heart would have easily chosen to stay and drown in the sea. I tried to gather up the anger that had pushed me out this far, but it was gone. My heart was a stone, and it wanted to sink. The sari agreed, but I had never been so thankful for my webbed fingers and toes. If I kept my legs kicking like a rhythmic motor, I could forget they existed. I wrapped my sari around my waist again, and tied it around my neck so that my arms were free. The sun set and darkness descended quickly. Lethargy filled my limbs like cement. Fear clasped hold of me and pulled. It gave my sari added weight and I dreamed that it was catching on coral after coral. When the fish brushed against my pumping legs, I gasped but pressed on. I focused my mind on the shore. Sand. Ground. Sand.

The waves pulled my body in all directions. As I got closer to the beach, I felt the tide pulling down and out. I thought I would be pulled apart. I reached the waves and rode them in. They pounded me into the sand like a small fish tangled in my sari net. I crawled up the beach. My eyes were filled with brine. I could barely see if there were other shadows around me. I managed to crawl up out of reach of the mountainous waves. I completely covered myself with my sari and the snarls of my hair. The night closed in around me. I fell asleep with my wet fingers curling into the sand.

Neela's hands were on me before I could open my crusted over and salted eyes. The sky was still dark, but her touch was as familiar as my own. The weakened aches of my battered body kept me at her mercy. I wanted to hit her. I wanted to claw the small hands that caressed mine like a child. I finally wiped my eyes and opened them to the dark shadow of my betrayer. I could only see a snake. Her skin was henceforth green to me. Her eyes yellow with narrow black slits. Her scales encircling me, claiming me, as she wrapped her body around me. Wherever she touched me, her cold skin burned. I still have the scars. Her tears shone like moonstones that swallowed stars. I smiled, pulled my hand out of hers to sign, *What do you want?*

She lifted her head, opened her arms and drew me in. I was a magnet, pulled to her by her snake charms. I let her hold me. My head rested between her thighs. My anger lifted my hand, made it slide up her skirt until it reached the place where she was hot and moist to the touch. My fingers found their way inside to where she had been taken by someone else. Her body rocked against me like the lover she used to be. Now she felt hollow like the place where my hand scratched at her insides, trying to pull something out. Prove she wasn't human, wasn't just a girl. I wanted to find the snake inside her that made her do what she did. Instead I made her want me again.

As the sky became purple and we could see people walking by the shore, I finally slid out of her like a snake. She had made me one, too. We curled up together in our nest, pretending to be two girls sitting in the sand, watching the sun rise out of the sea.

I tasted salt from the sea for weeks after Neela found me on the beach. Our passion wasn't the same. I missed the beginning so much that I played our story back in my dreams, in the pictures I drew on the pages of my secret journal, in the air when I was alone, on my skin along the rounded edges of the scars from my blisters. I layered hot turmeric paste on my scars, wishing they were still new.

TORN

Months after the day I rushed into the sea, three years after I first touched
my feet to Indian dirt, Neela and I were sitting on our newly-swept white
front steps. I was slowly drawing tiny henna leaves into the palm of her
hand.

We had been outside for hours. Children played in the street. Puppies
scampered around, fleeing from Ariyan as he kept guard over our yard. The
old woman herded her goats past us earlier, her face in its constant state
of consternation. She rarely looked in our direction or wagged her head
as most people did when they passed. Years ago, when we tried to catch
the young goats, she yelled at us, raising her stick. Now, when we saw her,
it made us smile and remember a time before the complications of skin,
touch, henna upon hands. Hands that knew where the edges of the sari
were and how to tuck beneath them, slip up and into—

I glanced up and thought I was seeing a mirage. My hand closed upon
the henna cone and accidentally released a misshaped blob onto Neela's
palm. I watched a man walk towards me. He had a giant hiker backpack on
his shoulders, red-rimmed blue eyes staring out from a red-bearded familiar
face. Father. He was wet from the sea. Salt glistened on his sunburned
cheeks. The beard was new, but he always had one after his sea expeditions.
Never this long, though. It made him look older. His body was tall and lean
like a fisherman.

For a long awkward moment, we stared at each other. I tried to envision
what he saw when he looked at me: my large dark blue eyes staring out from
eyelids traced with black, a blue jewel bindi sticker between my eyebrows
and red puja dust smeared above that; my hair pulled back into a long shiny
braid greased with coconut oil and decorated with jasmine flowers; my
green sari pulled tight across my breasts, bare feet barely sticking out from
under it; henna cone tight in my right fist, left hand holding Neela's right
hand as it rested across my knees. I'm sure he saw all these things, but what

did he think? Did he realise I had become something else altogether? I was not the daughter he'd left, but I read in his eyes that he had come to take me back. I hadn't realised I even missed him until he stood there, bending over to place his backpack on the ground beside us. I hated Mathi now. I hated Neela even more. But those were the things I was sorting out in my head. How dare he come back in the middle of my own mess of a life and expect me to walk away from all that I knew and loved?

Against the thoughts flooding my mind, my body rose and embraced him. Once his arms were around me, I felt the familiar sensation of safety, love, and protection, and yet I wanted to rebel against it. Tears flowed down my cheeks in black kajal rivers before I could call them back. He held me for longer than I wanted, but his arms were too strong for me to slip away. When he released me, he rested his heavy, sticky palms on my shoulders and kept staring at me as if I would disappear.

Why are you suddenly here? Why didn't you tell me anything? My signing caught him off guard, as I knew it would. He dropped his hands from my shoulders. His forehead scrunched up as he tried to remember. It was a language like any other, and I knew the years apart would make him forget most of it.

Sorry. I didn't have time to tell you. He managed sloppily, but I could read it.

I wasn't ready to talk to him yet, so I beckoned him to come inside with his bag. *Ammā's* hands flew up to her face when she saw him enter the kitchen. I could tell she wanted to hug him but her Tamil reservation barely held her back. She shook his hand roughly, and insisted that he sit down on the couch while she prepared tea and biscuits. He absolutely had to eat something and take tea, no excuses. I watched her head shake side-to-side.

While they were distracted, I stepped back outside. Neela was still sitting on the steps. She had barely acknowledged him when he passed her, and now she looked sick to her stomach. I sunk back down beside her. She turned to face me with more intensity than I had ever seen in her eyes. Tears were dried upon her cheeks. Streaks of salt mixed with the black kajal we both used. She rose fast and pulled me up with her. She dragged me into the back yard and pulled me into the bathing area. Bats scattered into the far corners as she slammed the door and locked it. She turned, crying again, and pressed her lips against mine so hard that it hurt.

I understood her ferocity, and I kissed her back just as hard. We paused for barely long enough to carefully unroll our bodies from our saris and hang them up where they wouldn't get wet or dirty. Then our shirts and underwear. Once we stood in the shadowy room, light spilling in from the cracks allowing us to see each other's naked forms in fragments, we stopped to stare. The splashes of light made her shoulders and hair shine and left her torso and legs muted and dark. In that moment, perhaps, I forgave her. We sank to the wet floor. She lay upon me the way she liked to, hands running up and down my sides. Beginning at my shoulders, she kissed my skin in a wavering line down to my belly. Her right hand covered my mouth, my lips pressed against the smudged, drying henna on its palm. It scratched them, but I didn't care. I held her hand there, the scent of henna filling my nose. After that day, whenever I used henna, I was brought back to Neela's hand over my mouth and her face between my legs.

With one hand in her hair, I let go completely for the first time. I bit into her hand as I felt a powerful surge throughout my body. Everything throbbed like the pulse of crashing waves until the sudden calm left me breathless and limp beneath her. Neela crawled up my sweating body and lay down heavily. Her face pressed into my neck and I felt her breath against my skin in ragged warm puffs. I wanted to freeze the moment and live inside it forever.

Dinner began a few hours later. The memory of it plays out like a theatre performance that I remember in snapshots.

Me—encased in bitter green wrapping paper: a trapped gift, still able to breathe.

Ammā with bowls in her arms: offerings.

Plates scattered on the low table. Bodies waiting around it: birds in a nest.

Father: newly dressed, washed, and miraculously, his beard shaved. Clean smooth face beneath the ocean eyes above. I couldn't look into them for fear of drowning.

Mathi—the tiger ready to pounce: staring with his feline eyes. Recording my emotions in a transparent notebook I could see behind the soft skin of his forehead.

Neela: her hands move like words in the air. *Are you doing ok? Do you like the food?*

Time gradually quickened to a normal speed as we ate. Father and Mathi both watched me. *Ammā's* lips continuously moved. She spoke to Father, to Mathi and Neela, to herself, to no one. Her eyes darted around in that nervous sort of way like when she looked for dust.

Neela barely ate because she kept talking with her hands: *Do you like the chapattis? I helped mother make them. Later, we can escape and go to the tea shop, maybe? Or are you very tired? Would you rather go to sleep early?*

I felt Father's eyes on her hands. He must have been impressed to see such fluency in a friend of mine. I didn't have many friends in Ireland, and none of them ever signed as well as Neela. I felt proud as I read her signs while I slowly pushed rice and vegetables into my mouth. I kept my hands busy so I didn't have to answer her. Easier to eat. Watch. Think. I thought I made it through the night until Mathi cornered me while I was putting dishes away in the kitchen. He moved behind me and blocked the doorway back to the living room. My hands were shaking when I signed, *What?!*

I had avoided him religiously since that day on the beach. I thought he had abandoned his wish to marry me, or at least, I hoped. He smiled down at me. His tiger paws moved. *I've been watching you. I know about you and Neela and I'm going to tell your father. If we marry, you can stay here. If we don't marry, you have to go with your father. I know you don't want that to happen.*

No! Stop your thoughts! Never! I will never marry you! I pushed my way past him and rushed back to Neela's side at the table.

I didn't think anyone saw our conversation, but Neela turned a questioning eye towards me and glared at Mathi as he came back in the room and sat down. I wasn't sure what to say or who to watch, so I sat there until it was okay for me to leave with Neela. Back to our room, under our protective sheet of elephants, I lay wishing I could follow the elephants away.

What were the moments that followed that fateful re-entry of Father back into my life? What did those short days contain? Her skin beneath the pads of my fingers. The tiny hairs of her slender arms. Breasts my head slept between, hiding.

I didn't want to see her words in sign. Or anyone's. Eyes downturned: I watched the red dirt moving below my feet. Ariyan's tiny face staring up into mine. Mathi's sandals—I ran when I saw them. But when Father's white feet pushed into my view, I had to raise my head. Make conversation. He had to relearn to sign fast. I didn't care. Didn't want to see words from the hands that would be taking me away. I did tell him. Eventually I had to. I signed, *You brought me here and now you're pulling me away from another place I love. This is my home now. I hate you!*

The words cut him. I saw his face wince. Wide eyes. Eyebrows pushed up. The wrinkled sweat of his forehead. I turned away. I ran off down the road with Ariyan following at my heels. Between the shops, the swinging coconuts, the rickshaws and mopeds. A place that I wanted to stay, even though I knew it wasn't mine. It had been my landscape for nearly three years. I was reborn here. It didn't matter that I didn't belong. I didn't belong anywhere. My lover, my Neela, was here. It was reason enough.

Neela didn't spend time with the boys or other girls anymore. Her attention, though I needed it, felt fueled by my impending absence. She was groping at me because I would be disappearing from her. Back to Ireland. There wasn't time within our last few days at their house for me to analyse the meaning behind her caresses, so I took them. Greedy like a much smaller child. We sneaked into the toilets at school to make love. When I stopped going to school, she did, too, and we had our bathing room and the canyons for our pleasures.

My body represented the cruelty of fate and time. Neela tore at it. Her nails carved red lines into my skin that I prayed would never fade or heal. Violent. Primal. We became animals. At night we rubbed oil over the claw marks across our backs, and smiled because at least we were fighting. If Father had to take me away, take her away from me, I would rip us both to shreds before we could be torn apart.

The countdown of days—

Five: coconut juice dripping down the side of her face.

Four: the red edges of the canyons reflected in her eyes.

Three: rose syrup on our hands, sticking them together.

Two: afternoon tea spilled onto the soft hairs of her arm. Licked off indiscreetly.

The night before I left, *Ammā* made a small feast. She cried while we ate it. I was surprised because she rarely showed much emotion. Father glanced up at her repeatedly while trying to look like he didn't notice her tears as he ate vigorously. Mathi carefully and slowly pushed food into his mouth while surveying each of us. Neela and I were the only ones who appeared normal. Although we were the ones dying inside. I tried to eat but my stomach was full of something, as if a creature had crawled inside me and was stuck within its thin sac, pushing around, kicking. Beside me, Neela's hands told me multiple things at once: *Tomorrow you're going to leave early and mother will probably force me to go to school. How can I do that without—*

Her hands fell down to her lap in mid-sentence. One rose to push more rice into her mouth, with some of it falling. Ariyan ate it off the floor and ran out before *Ammā* could scream. She was still crying, so she wouldn't have noticed anyway.

In bed we lay like dolls. The light from the candle made the air pulse in an orange heartbeat. Fear crept around in the shadows like a predator on the fringes of the room, waiting to pounce, patient. Neela moved first. Her tears interrupted the black lines of her eyelids, creating blackened watery rivers running down her face. I thought of running away. Anything to stay here, with her. Why couldn't I have been born a snake? Like Neela. Able to slither. My doll hand came up stiffly. Fingers cracked as they reached to touch her face. My fingertips grasping at the drops, overcome with thirst. Dolls coming to life, we crumbled together. The wind of our union blew the candle out—leaving us in the dark.

Father and I waited for our taxi. The sun left us, sudden grey clouds spread over the sky. The monsoon wasn't due yet, but it began to pour. I sat on the steps in my favourite sari—black, orange, and gold. My largest gold flower nose ring gleaming, proclaiming me Indian. Saffron dust on my forehead: a blessing. Neela's right hand in my left. While staring into each other's eyes, we instinctively reached up to our necks with opposite hands— grasped the tiny silver Ganesh charms we both had on strings in prayer. As if Ganesh could protect us more than he already had. Longer. Together.

The taxi arrived late but it was intact. Father and the driver lifted our bags into the trunk. *Ammā*'s body shook with sobs. Mathi stood stiffly off to the side. A tiger defeated. Neela and I almost kissed, our heads leaned, our bodies hummed with energy we couldn't possibly express. We embraced instead. Her breasts pressed fiercely against my own and I never wanted them to separate, but we had to. Eyes watched all around. Father was shaking hands with Mathi, nodding to *Ammā*. All I could think was: I had lived with her for over three years, and in three more, I would be eighteen. I would be old enough to come and find her again. We separated. I signed, *I promise I'll come back to you. I'll love you forever.*

I'll love you forever. She was crying.

Upon reaching Madras, we boarded a train to New Delhi. As it moved slowly along the tracks, my body shifted back and forth ever so slightly. Father was a stone across from me—his eyes fixed on some point outside the dusty windows. I looked down at my body—beaten. Bruised. A hole cut through its centre. The tight sari top kept my heart from sliding out. I would have to wear it forever.

Down a dark street in New Delhi, I found a tree with the saffron powder sticking to it in a clump. I wasn't sure what type of tree it was. I touched the wide trunk that had been painted with a stripe of white around its base, so that people would see it at night as they drove past. I felt the roughness of the bark and fingered the tattered fabrics hanging from it. I took my finger, dipped it into the deep red powder, and closed my eyes to press the sacred dust into the space on my forehead above my bindi. I found a patch of white powder on the same tree, and drew a short line beneath the saffron on my forehead. Strength. Power. Kali.

In the window of our hostel, I meditated until the sun began to rise—a red ball of flame in an orange sky. I felt Father waking up behind me and kept my eyes ahead. I wanted my last moments in India to be mine. I drew an invisible circle around my body so that nothing would disturb that dawning of the day I had to leave this land, this extension of myself, its beauty of wildly painted temples and trees with branches that curved straight back into the Earth.

I had barely begun to understand India or myself. For the first time, India wasn't overshadowed by Neela. It spread before me with its dirty streets, opened wounds, opened Earth. India welcomed me into its canyons, red dirt and red gods, but now I was rising up—flying away—and all I wanted was to rush back down into the dirt, into India like a banyan. The roots that arched into the air, dancing, circling each other, sprouting wide green leaves as they dissolve into thinner and thinner tendrils. The banyan's branches clamouring together, tripping over each other in their slow growth outwards from the original trunk, and back into the ground. Perhaps they joined the real roots below the dirt—a circle. Completion. I wanted roots like that, too.

I T A L Y

Canals: spilling through gaps between the roads.

Black boats: dark crescent moons floating on their backs.

White masks: cracked and yellowed, silver painted
mouths.

Heavy gold rings on doors: hanging from the jaws of small
lions.

Pink-flowered windowsills: old women peering down,
inquisitive.

CITY OF MAZES

Father led me down narrow maze-like streets across the canals on arched white bridges. The buildings were sculpted in columns, stone faces peering out, pink and yellow flowers bursting from their cracks. Colours like faded Hindu temples, the same crumbling walls and small windows. My hand reached up, fingers trying to feel inside my nose to see if it had closed again. Why was there suddenly nothing to smell? No pollution or rotten fish or fried foods or the ripe smell of sweat. Nothing until the burst of fragrance from a flower shop. I had forgotten that the smell of European countries could never match that of India.

Our heavy bags weighed us down. People stared as they passed by in massive crowds. This was Venice. I never believed the stories: a city that floated on water. A place where canals were used as often as streets. Boat taxis. Boat buses. A probable haven for a water-lover like myself or Father. The only problem—he lied. I hadn't paid attention in New Delhi. I assumed Venice was a stopover, not a destination. I imagined a small fin sticking out of Father's back. His hand against my palm: leather. Blue vellum. Blue like his eyes and the sea that must have made him, too. Father the shark. Selfish. Deceptive. Circling me.

I was supposed to be his pilot fish. Swim close againt his large body. Faithful. Feed on his leftovers. Symbiotic to his needs. I looked down at my own skin and I found no black and white markings, just an irremovable sari top beneath a loose *punjabi* the colour of blood. My hair hung down over it, and the sun trapped inside the strands made them shine red and gold. Under those carefully chosen fabrics, carefully combed hairs, I felt my own skin shifting, turning silver. Shining. Dark with longing for water. Submersion. Neela. Mother. I wasn't Father's pilot fish. I was like Mother. I was his prey. And he didn't know it. He didn't want to see anything but his own desires.

We arrived at an old faded brick building squeezed between rows of other homes on either side. It had windows with pink flowers. Four rows up was the sky. There was a balcony on its roof, like ours in India. This one felt too high. My body was numb. My muscles were thick with fatigue. They wanted to be wet, to float upwards rather than walk. Instead I followed Father through the deep brown door with an old man's face staring down at me from the stone arch above it. It looked real, though his head was three times smaller than my own and clearly part of the grey stone. It guarded this place like a spirit, like Ariyan.

My legs took careful steps up a narrow stairway behind Father. My hands grasped the straps of my backpack, thankful to be free of the rough skin of his palm. Our apartment was on the third floor. I was glad it wasn't higher. There were two balconies, one in the living room and one in the master bedroom. Windows overlooked a residential back canal. The kitchen reminded me of a walk-in wardrobe. The living room had walls the colour of mint rice, an oversized black couch, and off-white painted wood floors. The door shut behind us. I looked up into Father's eyes. His hands moved to sign something but mine moved faster. *Stop*, I signed, *No more lies.*

Ok, ok. It was a long journey. You can take the room with the balcony. Try to get some sleep.

I narrowed my eyes. He was right. I was so exhausted I knew I would fall asleep within minutes of lying down. Sleep and Father conspired against me. I couldn't let them win. *No! Tell me now! Why are we here?*

He lowered his pack to the floor, sighed, and began, *I'm not ready to go to Ireland. I thought you'd like it here. I want to write a book about my studies and I thought this would be a good place to write.*

I wanted to hit him. Run. Scream. Leap off of our brand new balconies into the dirty canal. Instead, I replied, *You you you! It's always all about you! I'm nothing! I'm just a concept to you, I'm not real. So you're nothing to me either. Fuck you!*

Before he could respond to the first profanity he had ever seen me use, I turned, dragged my backpack into the room with the nice balcony, and slammed the door behind me.

I opened my bag and pulled out a tapestry of elephants marching in lines. Neela and I had gone to Pondy and found the same sheets we had on our bed. Something I could carry with me always. Elephants to guard me. I wrapped it around myself, curled up on the bare mattress, and fell asleep.

In my dreams, I swam with Mother in her seal body. Followed her down below the islands, down through the long eelgrass. The grass felt silky where it touched me. I had to spread it apart and swim through the water jungle towards Mother's home. I almost made it there. She swam faster as I tried to keep up, tried to keep her dark form in view—

Squinting from the brightness of the sun through the windows, I wiped my face and realised there was no eelgrass around me. Soft sheets instead. Across the room: a small glass door and my new balcony behind it. The clock beside me glared a large red 3:17. I had slept nearly twenty-four hours. My body must not have wanted to be here either. Even in sleep, it pulled me down into the sea.

Holding my sheet tight around me, I walked over to the door. I fished a pair of sunglasses out of my bag. I never wore them in India. In Venice, I wanted to hide. Behind those dark lenses, I stepped out onto the balcony. Leaning against the black railing, I felt the ripples on the canal below me flow up under my skin. A cool wave pushing the layers of my epidermis upwards from underneath, somewhere between flesh and bone. Urging my hairs to lift up and dance. Moving along the hidden veins, glands, nerves, down into my fingers, back up along my arms, curving around my shoulder blades, pouring into the organ beating against my chest, pushing the streams of blood up through the arch of aorta, out along the arteries. All this from the closer proximity to water. Any water was a way home.

This canal was narrow, barely wide enough for two boats to pass each other. It curved out of sight in both directions. If only I knew which way was out of the maze: away from the islands and into the sea. Across the canal to my right was one of the many courtyards. The golden cross of a church rose up above the other buildings. This area was mostly made up of apartments: laundry hanging on strings, plant-filled windowsills with old women staring down. Inside my skin, my blood thickened and slowed to a faint pumping as my heart transformed into iron—a weight that wanted me to fall off the balcony, topple into the water below and sink. I tossed my sheet back into the room. Laid down my sunglasses and leaped into the empty stretch of canal below.

It was not Lord Byron's time of nightly naked swims. The water teemed with modern pollutants. Warm from the boat motors that constantly rumbled through. Tiny bits of trash and paper floated around me. It was dirty, but my new apartment and the closer proximity to Father felt worse.

My *punjabi* was easier to swim in than a sari.

Underwater, the contamination hurt my eyes; it passed over my skin like chemicals tingling. I swam quickly down the length of the canal. Turned right when it turned. Swam deeper when I could see the bottoms of the gondolas cruising above. Eventually the toxic waste lessened and I knew I was reaching the sea. From below, I watched boats passing back and forth. I noticed a row of boats docked to my left. Needing to breathe, I turned towards them.

It was difficult to find a place to surface without being seen. I weaved my body like a fish between the long wooden legs of the docks. Poked my head up—a curious seal between the black floating slabs of gondolas. I noticed a tiny canal pushing its way through the cobblestone streets back into the city. There was a place I could pull myself up beneath a pretty white bridge arching from one section of street to another. My body slumped up onto the land. Was it land? Instead of dirt, Venice was made of stone and cement. I wondered what was here before humans built this floating city. The boats chased away the fish. I sat against the cold white wall. My clothes weren't drying in the shadow of the buildings. I began to shiver. I rose awkwardly to my feet and braved the crowds so that I could walk in the sun.

My feet carried me for hours. I wasn't used to getting lost so easily. From nearly anyplace on the roadside of my Irish home, I could see the rest of town sprawled out around me. Here the men prowled with cat-like grins, women carried rosaries in their hands, tourists pointed with their curious fingers, snapping pictures everywhere. Tiny shops were filled with masks and sculpted glass. Coffee was brewed instead of chai. The scents of warm pastries and pizza made my stomach rumble.

I followed the streets that were closest to the outside of the islands, where I could watch the sea extend in calm ripples to the line of the horizon. My clothes dried but I could smell the trash on them. I felt embarrassed. But who did I even know here? Nobody. It was nice. Strangers speaking foreign tongues. Moving lips all around. No heads moving side-to-side. Muted colours. Pastels instead of bright or dark. Pink. Light blue. Sea green. Yellow. Faded like old parchment. Masks instead of gods. I eventually had to walk into the inner streets of Venice so that I could find my way back to that room, that balcony. Sleep once again. I felt my stomach lurching as I took one step and another as I tried to block out the scents of food.

My skin burned along its edges in scattered spots. Forest fires. My right arm smelled of rotten fish, my left of gasoline. My organs and blood wanted to join my skin. My mind felt huddled in the dark of a polluted canal. My steps wavered and I bumped into people. I felt them glaring and imagined their mouths speaking to me so I kept my eyes on my feet. Sometimes I wished I could tattoo the words I'M DEAF across my forehead.

I almost jumped back into yet another residential narrow canal, figuring I had better luck finding my way underwater, when I noticed a street show going on in the next courtyard. I watched a boy riding a one-wheeled bike in a circle while juggling shiny red and yellow balls. People stood around or passed along the edges of the shops on either side of him. I found an out-of-the-way place to rest my legs and sit against the sidewall of a café.

Immediately after I sat down, a beautiful reddish-tan large dog came over to me. His small black nose ran over the length of my legs and arms before burying itself in the fabric of my shirt below my waist. I had to pull hard to lift his head from between my legs. It was the first time I had smiled in days. The sudden crack of my veneer mouth brought tears to my eyes. The unexpected joy left a bitter taste in my mouth. I wasn't supposed to be happy here.

The dog had no concept of such things. He twisted his head and licked my lips as they quivered in that uncomfortable space between a smile and a frown. Staring into his shiny brown eyes flecked with hues of orange and yellow like trapped sunlight, I felt at home. Dogs reminded me of seals. I hugged him. He turned his body towards the boy on the bike while sitting heavily between my legs, pushing them apart like familiar pillows. He started licking my bare left foot. It tickled, but it felt cleaner as he licked it. I threaded my fingers through the dog's fur as I watched the show.

I noticed that the boy on the bike kept looking towards me, or rather, towards my new friend. When I realised it must be his dog, my hands automatically moved out of his fur. My newly heated palms tingled with desire to keep touching the dog, but my mind kept them back. He wasn't my dog to touch, and this wasn't India, where nobody cared about the dogs. This boy cared. I could see it in the arch of his eyebrows as he checked me over, probably writing me off as a poor street urchin that shouldn't be sitting practically underneath his wonderful canine.

His eyes were dark brown like an Indian. His skin was the colour of honey. I couldn't tell if it was a tan or natural. He was darker than Italians, but not as dark as most Indians. A few black curling ringlets escaped from beneath his hard hat and swung back and forth across his cheeks. He wore a tight navy blue bodysuit, short-sleeved and cut off at the knees. His body moved in rhythm with the bike. He lit the ends of a stick he was twirling so that it became a double-sided torch spinning in the air. The flames dazzled me and I forgot my resolve not to pet the dog.

Meanwhile, the dog had fallen asleep, his head on my calf, probably intoxicated from the chemicals it had licked off my foot. I was a bad influence already. My eyes grew heavy from the calm of the dog's slow breathing.

I jumped when the dog leaped to his feet at the boy's approach. The sky had become shades of dark violet and deep blue. Streetlights were already glowing yellow. The boy leaned down towards me, hat-less, tiny rivers of sweat running down the sides of his face. Water bottle in hand. Mouth moving. Damn. How could I convey? I did my usual waving of my hands, shaking of my head, pointing to my ears, and blocking them with my palms. His eyes widened, his hands mimicking mine, also pointing to my ears. I nodded.

We stared at each other for a long, strangely comfortable moment. Until I raised my eyebrows and pretended to write on my palm, trying to ask him if he had paper. Thumbs up and a wide grin was his reply. He darted off to a cluster of bags and the remains of his show gadgets, still scattered off to one side of the emptying square. He came back with a pen and a notebook covered in abstract doodles. Finding an empty page, he wrote: SCUSA, MI CHIAMO PETRU.

I knew it would be in Italian. I could guess his meaning, but I knew I wouldn't be able to guess much else, so I tried writing: SORRY, MY NAME IS LA- I had to stop for a minute. It was the first time I realised I had to use my old name again. My Indian name didn't fit here, it wasn't—me? - FIONNUALA. DO YOU KNOW ENGLISH? (EST-CE QUE PARLES ANGLAIS?)

I had learned some French in school, so I figured maybe he would know that if he didn't know English. I didn't expect the look of utter joy sweep across his face as he grabbed back the pen. YOU VERY SMART ! TU PARLES FRANÇAIS! AND ENGLISH! VERY GOOD. MY ENGLISH NOT SO GOOD. I AM FROM CORSICA. I SPEAK CORSICAN, FRENCH, AND ITALIAN. SOME ENGLISH. WHERE ARE YOU FROM ?

IRELAND. I gave him the pen before I could write any more. I wasn't ready to discuss my real country.

OH! I HEAR IRELAND IS A BEAUTIFUL COUNTRY, LIKE CORSICA, ONLY MUCH MORE RAIN AND COLD. YES?

I nodded. He made me smile because he was so carefree.

We wrote back and forth into the darkness, leaning into a circle of light from the streetlamp above, each of us petting his dog. His dog's name was Casanova. That made me smile, too. He called himself a gypsy, but he was only seventeen. I asked him where his family was, and he said they were back on his island. He had traveled to Venice with friends, gypsies, and street performers. He knew the mimes and the men in the masks I had seen earlier by the sea. I told him very little. Father recently moved me here. I ran off, got lost. I fell into the canal, got stinky.

At which point he gave me a long, concerned look, and wrote: IT IS TOO LATE TO FIND YOUR HOME NOW. YOU COME WITH ME, I KEEP YOU SAFE. YOU CAN HAVE SHOWER, BED FOR YOU TO SLEEP, THEN TOMORROW WE FIND YOUR HOME. VENICE AT NIGHT IS NOT SO SAFE FOR YOUNG GIRLS. YOU ARE LUCKY TO FIND ME AND CASANOVA! S'IL TE PLAÎT, D-ACCORD?

My head nodded again. I sensed that he was a good person. He and his dog were like one creature. Both looked relieved as if they were sudden protectors called to a job. I had never met a boy like him before. On the way to his home, I walked his bike while he carried his bags. Even with bags hanging from his shoulders, his feet skipped as they walked. Nobody walked that way in India. I could do it here, too, couldn't I? I could walk that way, kick my legs up, laugh loudly if I dared. I could—

Not yet. My Indian limbs stayed straight. Walked carefully one step in front of the other.

His apartment was empty when we arrived, though the remains of his roommates were everywhere: dirty dishes balanced on the edges of tables next to sketches of people's faces or boats, body-less costumes limply draped themselves over the edges of the couches and chairs, open books scattered on the floor. We tiptoed across the debris towards a closed door on the other side of the room.

Petru's bedroom had one large mattress on the floor and piles of sleeping bags curled up on it. Casanova immediately ran over to it and nested himself in the pile. A long row of books lined the back wall. Most were in French or Italian, with a few in English: *Le Fantôme De L'Opéra. The Complete Works of Shakespeare. Le Città Invisibili. Les Misérables. Harry Potter.*

He rustled through some bags in a corner of the room. I waited, having leaned his bike against the side wall. This was a place where I could live—a home; messy, yet inviting. Petru turned to me with a T-shirt and shorts in his hands. I took them awkwardly. He pointed to himself, then pointed to the mess in his room and made elaborate motions with his arms. I liked his way of expressing that he was going to organise his room. I began to sway my head side-to-side and caught myself. With a forced nod up and down, I followed his lead to the bathroom.

It was as cluttered as the rest of the apartment. Soaps, shampoos, conditioners lay open and scattered on the bottom of the antique claw-footed tub. The shower curtain was torn but functional. I stepped into the stream of water with my *punjabi* on and peeled it off while the clean water pulled the chemicals out. The smell of soap was strange but comforting. My black sari top stayed on because it still felt like a part of my own skin. When I stepped out, I had to find a blow dryer for it. The thin fabric dried faster than I thought possible. I dried my hair a little too. The hot air reminded me of India. I let it blow into my face for a while.

Finally, I opened the bathroom door to find the place still empty except for Petru cooking in the kitchen. The scent of basil was overpowering. It made me want to curl up in the sleeping bag nest with Casanova. It allowed me to forget my discomfort in shorts. Nobody—besides Neela—had seen my legs in years. They were long white slim things that didn't seem to belong to me. My arms were so tan. Covered in brownish freckles. Shoulders now black and made of fabric. Black cotton breasts. No longer touched. Kissed. Petru was too occupied to notice my long pause in the bathroom doorway. He smiled and accidentally did the sign for *food*. Everyone could guess that one. I was sick of nodding in the straight up and down way, so I smiled and lifted my arms that carried the wet *punjabi*. He pointed to the balcony and acted out someone hanging clothes on the railings. I couldn't believe how easy his body found ways to communicate to me. I ran for the pen and paper he'd left on his bedroom floor and wrote: YOU ACT AS A MIME SOMETIMES, TOO?

He gave me a guilty nod and it explained everything. Mimes were easy to comprehend! That was it. I felt lucky. I had a friend again. Is that what he was? Could a boy be a friend to a girl? It was a hard concept to grasp. Something large and Neela-shaped stood in the way. A dark sari spread out over the sand. Across my eyes. Her hands. Henna. Dark green chunks. Skin turning deep orange beneath. Tiny sketched leaves. Curled petals.

The spaghetti he made was the first thing I had eaten since we arrived the day before. I didn't realise how hungry I was until the smell of the frying tomatoes, garlic, and fresh basil made my stomach growl like a small monster tumbling in its stretchy sac. I ate a huge bowl of it with freshly grated Italian cheese without even thinking of Indian food. This food was warm in a different way. Less harsh. More filling. He gave me half a glass of red wine and I almost fell asleep in my empty bowl with Casanova's sneaky head upon my lap. I jumped when I felt Petru's arms lifting me up off the couch, but quickly relaxed again once he laid me down in the nest covering me with its thick wrappings. I was asleep with Casanova's warm furry body nuzzled against mine in minutes. The door shut, we were left in the dark. My first night of sleep without the elephants marching across my sheets.

GOLD-PAINTED TREE

The next morning I opened my eyes to an empty room. My limbs were tangled in dark blue sheets. Bits of reddish fur, but the dog that shed them was gone. Gradually my life came into focus and I remembered: Casanova. Petru. Father? He was probably worried. I remembered I was supposed to look for him today. Go find my apartment. That balcony. Elephant sheets. All I wanted was the sunglasses.

I opened the door of the room to find Petru and Casanova on the balcony just beyond where we ate the night before. Casanova jumped up and ran over to me. Ears straight up. Nose in the air. Tail moving side-to-side, wagging his entire bottom. Petru looked up from a book he was reading and waved. I walked over and sat on the stone floor of the balcony, allowing the canal ripples to move up under my skin yet again. It reminded me of the rooftop of my home in India. Petru held a deep red cloth-bound book in his hands. The short lines wavering down the centre of the pages told me it was poetry. The accents above the words told me it wasn't English. His hair was tied back in a ponytail. His eyes had bits of light caught in their darkness as he smiled at me.

You sleep? He signed without realizing he was signing.

Yes. I signed and nodded.

He jumped up suddenly and ran inside. A few minutes later he came back with hot coffee, bread, butter, jam. The strong coffee was a bitter change from sweetened chai. I added extra sugar and milk. It tasted better, but it would still take me a while to adapt. It woke my whole body like a drug. I wanted to jump back into the water below, but I wasn't prepared to share my secret with Petru yet. Nor was I prepared to leap into a crowded canal. We faced one of the touristy areas of the city. Across the wide stretch of water was the casino halfway through its restoration. A long picture of a painted half of the building hung down over one side. The other side was completed in white stone, pillars, small faces. Private boats, gondolas, and taxis passed back and forth between us.

I looked back at Petru as he reached for pen and paper: YOU WANT TO GO AND FIND YOUR FATHER NOW? GO HOME?

I shook my head automatically. With him eyeing me with concern, I wrote: I HATE MY FATHER. I DON'T REALLY WANT TO GO BACK. BUT I DON'T KNOW WHAT ELSE TO DO. CAN I STAY WTH YOU ONE OR TWO MORE DAYS? YOU'VE BEEN SO NICE TO ME.

He sat and stared at me. He nodded slowly, half-smiled. I knew I'd have to explain more eventually. I must have looked like a troubled kid. He asked me my age and I had to think before I wrote—15.

It was July, and school wasn't until September. I had an entire summer of possible imprisonment by Father. Petru had left his own family, but it didn't seem like he was happy about that. Would Father try to find me? I wasn't sure. I grabbed the paper: HOW CAN I MAKE MONEY? DO YOU KNOW OF A JOB? FOR SUMMER?

He lit up and wrote: I CAN TEACH YOU MIME. YOU ALREADY KNOW HOW TO SPEAK WITH HANDS! YOU MAKE MUCH MONEY! TOURISTS LIKE GIRLS!

I loved it: mask, white face paint, loose clothes, rags, props. I could disappear. Instead of searching for my apartment, Petru gave me a tour of Venice. He said we could watch the mimes and street shows. Tomorrow I could try it. It looked easy. The hardest part was the heat of the rags and layers of clothes, but that wouldn't even bother me. Venice still felt cool to me after India. Petru and I walked hand-in-hand through the crowds so that I wouldn't get lost.

He let me borrow some euros to get sunglasses. I found large ones with blue circular frames. I was so happy to be back in the dark that I squeezed my arms around Petru's waist, held my face against his chest, and slipped away before he could hug me back. I ran ahead with Casanova as he paid for them and rushed to catch up. We went to the Rialto and the train station, then down through vacant alleys and streets. White church. Faded red brick church. Grey stone church. As if each one was for a different god. Crosses dotted the corners of my eyes like traffic signals. A black fountain here. A grey one there. Pigeons drank from their arched transparent streams.

We walked across to the far side where I had climbed out of the canal the day before. Stepped over pools in between crowds of people feeding armies of pigeons in front of St. Mark's Basilica. Its outsides were covered in half-circle shaped-paintings with backgrounds of gold, stone statues dancing around their edges in their own frozen puppet show. Black sculpted horses above the main door, above the lines of people wanting to go inside where ceilings and walls were covered with gold. It looked like an inside-out duplicate of Maduri's golden temple. Does everybody worship gold? I couldn't tell the difference between the churches that were in every square of Venice and the temples of India. Who were these intangible gods?

Petru wasn't Christian. That surprised me. He didn't know what to believe since he was programmed into Christianity his entire life. I felt the same. Yet there were myths on Corsica, nature stories, like the ones I knew from Ireland. We both related more to those. I remembered the white sculpture of Mary that sat up on the cliffs on the way to *Dún Chaoin*. The narrow road curved against the grey stone high above the crashing waves. We used to walk along it. The white figure of Mary always seemed lonely to me, even though her view of *Coum Dhíneol, Tráigh a' Choma*, and *Na hOileáin* was my favourite view in all of Ireland. Like the stone faces in Venice. The stone gods in India. How do people believe in things they can't even touch?

Petru's hand was getting sweaty inside my own. We stopped to sit under a bridge and ate stuffed pizza with spinach and ricotta. It was wonderful and rich, but I wanted spices. Heaping piles of rice on a banana leaf. Chai. My legs didn't want to walk any further. I wanted to flop like a seal back to Petru's apartment. Instead he lifted me up easily and walked back through empty side streets. It felt weird that he kept carrying me. I didn't realise how small I was in body. Indians were skinnier and shorter. I wondered if the spirit of the people here made them vast. They seemed able to do anything they desired. I wanted that, too.

I woke the next morning to a wet dog tongue lapping at my lips. My eyes opened to Casanova's big black nose and concerned eyes. I embraced his rust-coloured fur. Slowly got used to the change in place. Gradually came back to Venice. I was exhausted from traveling every time I closed my eyes. Backwards. Forwards. Backwards again. But today was the day I would learn how to mime. I got up quickly.

After a cup of coffee, we made our way down to the Rialto, where many of Petru's friends worked. The other boy who lived in the apartment knew of me already. All of them greeted me with their mime smiles, some white-faced, some from behind elaborate masks. Some of their masks were blue like the Hindu gods, though their dress was either flowing rags or elaborate gowns and suits from the sixteenth century. Gold-trimmed. Bright yellow satin. Skirts were round like the sun.

We wandered through the squares on either side of the Rialto Bridge, watching the mimes. Some stood alone like statues leaning against a wall or a cane. Others interacted with each other: dancing, fixing each other's costumes, playing music. Tourists were pulled towards the movements or the elaborate masks, but they were also mystified by the ones who didn't move at all. The stillness amidst the crowds and excitement was unsettling, amazing to watch, especially the ones standing in the hot sun. Only their sweat moved, barely discernable, beneath masks, creeping out of the cracks in their painted faces. I wanted to be one of the statues.

Petru's eyebrows wrinkled as he sighed and wrote: TO BE STILL IS TOO HARD TO START WITH. EASIER TO MOVE. FOR YOU, TO SIGN. MORE FUN.

But I wouldn't let him talk me out of it. I wanted to try it. ONE DAY.

He couldn't say no. We used my idea of a tree, and we found the mask I had seen the day before. Painted leaves of gold, green, and brown covered the entire face except for the bottom of the nose and around the mouth. Lips painted silver. While I held it up, superimposing it upon my own face, Petru tying the string at the back of my head, I felt complete in a way I never had before. Completed by a costume. The webs between my fingers tingled at its falseness. I embraced it because it wasn't permanent, it wasn't true. I didn't want truth anymore.

The clothes were easy. We used a sleeveless off-white shirt and painted more leaves on it, added golden shimmer and sparkles. Rough painted edges. Then we found an off-white flowing skirt and covered it with dark brown branches fringed in silver. We dusted the skin of my bare arms in more gold. Looking into the dusty mirror of Petru's bathroom, Petru and Casanova on either side of me, a couple other mimes peeking in from the doorway: I felt beautiful. Behind the mask, I could allow tears to escape, barely altering the gold-painted skin they had to cross before dripping down my hidden cheeks. I wasn't sure if I was crying because of my costume or because I had finally removed the sari top and felt my heart slide down over my bare skin, past my underwear, down the inside of my legs to escape through the floor, through the Earth, back to Neela. I had become a shell. A heartless husk of a girl. This tree was my new identity.

We left in the late afternoon, so that Petru could perform his show a few streets down from the train station. I positioned myself a few blocks down from him, near a fruit market and fairly empty square with a white stone church. We put fake leaves around the edges of a dark brown basket for people to put money into. Petru warned me that I may not get much within only a few hours. I just wanted to stand there. Frozen. Watch the people passing with their shopping bags and their laughter. Venice was a lighthearted city. It took the colourful intensity of India and transformed it into a carnival. Colours painted in joy rather than severity.

Casanova was torn between us for a moment, but he stayed with his master. I wanted the time alone anyway. People were already watching me when I stopped next to a café. I picked a spot to the left of the church, beyond the cluster of fruit stands and souvenir racks. This side of the courtyard was relatively empty. People strolled through it after buying fruits or vegetables, or for a quick cappuccino at the café. Petru taught me that this was a good place because tourists or locals would have extra change already in their hands.

The first pose I tried wasn't complicated enough to attract much attention. I stood still against the wall. Branches were painted on the insides of my arms, so I held them open but kept them down because I knew it would hurt if I tried to hold one arm in the air for too long. My head rested against the wall, eyes staring at the people passing. The first hour left me with a mere handful of coins, but everyone looked at me. The peace and stillness of such immobility proved not to be as wonderful as I imagined. I was bored. I tried lifting one arm, placed my hand on my shoulder so that my elbow pointed diagonally upwards and my cheek rested on the top of my hand. I knew it would hurt after a while, but I figured the pain would help make it interesting. I liked how the branches of my right arm could bend in such a way.

More people came over. Some tilted their heads like mine. Children smiled and touched the painted leaves of my skirt with miniature hands that parents snatched away. People tried to get me to move or speak. Oddly enough, nobody could tell if I was deaf or hearing. For the first time, I didn't have to be either. Tourists leaned in as closely as they dared. Their lips moved, but I didn't move. I didn't notice that I had stopped breathing completely until my chest felt tight and I had to take a huge breath that caused my breasts to expand under the scrutiny of one young boy whose eyes bulged with curiosity and embarrassment that made me smile beneath my mask. Thankfully invisible.

Petru couldn't take his eyes off me once he entered the square. Casanova finally noticed me when they got closer, and ran up to me with his tail wagging maniacally. He automatically stuck his nose up the bottom of my skirt and the wetness of it against my bare calves nearly made me move. I was trying to impress Petru, so I kept still. I didn't move until he gestured to me with worry in his eyes. I understood why when I finally brought my right arm down. Pain shot through it as if it had been still for months instead of an hour. I felt humbled when I wanted to cry. Petru immediately rubbed my arm. The human touch felt strange after the hours of solitude. His hands were soft yet firm and they massaged the muscles in my arm, helping my blood to flow back through it. No one had touched me like that since Neela. Yet because Petru was so genuinely nice, I felt guilty that it was still her hands I wanted. I reached up and stopped him after a few minutes. It had helped but I still couldn't move that arm or hold anything with it. It would take time. I wasn't discouraged at all.

Petru stopped to write: ARE YOU SURE YOU ARE OK? DID YOU REALLY STAND THAT WAY FOR 2 HOURS? SINCE YOU GOT HERE?

I was tempted to write YES, but guilt forced me to admit: NO. JUST ONE HOUR. BEFORE I HAD BOTH ARMS DOWN, BUT IT WAS BORING AND NOT MANY PEOPLE CAME TO GIVE ME MONEY, SO I CHANGED POSITION AND MANY MORE PEOPLE GAVE MONEY!

Thankfully, he was still impressed. We counted the money and found that I made 18 euros and 30 cents. I was overjoyed since it was only two hours of standing there, and that seemed like a considerable amount of cash. I could already give Petru all of it and it covered the cost of my mask and the sunglasses! I still needed to make twenty or so more for the clothes and paint we used, but maybe I would the next day.

He wouldn't take my money. He wrote: NO. THIS IS YOUR FIRST DAY'S WORK. IT MUST BE YOURS. YOU CAN PAY ME BACK LATER, NEXT WEEK, WHEN YOU HAVE MADE MUCH MORE. OK? I WOULD NEVER TAKE YOUR FIRST DAY'S MONEY. SO WHAT DO YOU WANT TO DO NOW? WE CAN GO OUT, OYSTERS HERE ARE AMAZING, OR CAPPUCCINO? WE MUST CELEBRATE!

I was tired. I didn't want to ruin his fun, so I smiled and we brought our things back to his apartment. I changed back into my *punjabi*, but I kept the sari top folded and carefully placed it beneath my tree costume in the corner of Petru's bedroom and walked away from it without looking back.

We left his apartment in a group: Petru, Casanova, me, Petru's Italian roommate, Giovanni, and another friend of theirs, Michel. They both looked naked to me without their makeup and classical suits. They also caught on fast to communicating with me via mime and paper. JUST CALL ME GIO was the first thing Giovanni wrote as I admired his hands. They looked as if they had been sculpted and painted a perfect shade of tan. His sly eyes traveled over me as I looked away, pretending not to notice. A Polish girl, Zosia, also lived in the apartment, but she was out that night already. I hadn't met her yet. My body instinctively leaned down towards Casanova, because my desire for a girl had made me shy away from the boys.

Once I volunteered that I had never tried the Italian ice cream delicacy they called *gelato,* Petru led me to a tiny stand next to the train station. I tried a scoop of pistachio and a scoop of tiramisu. Both of them melted in my mouth with flavors of nut and coffee, hints of chocolate and cinnamon. I finished the cone in minutes. Petru glowed at my reaction as he led me away from the stand, down by the black waters with radiant balls of yellow lights dancing off them as the boats gently passed by. It was strange to be out at night without beggars, or people staring or trying to talk to me. I was able to sit peacefully with Casanova's head in my lap, the boys wrapped in an animated dialogue I didn't care to permeate. For the first time in Venice, I was happy.

Later on, Petru and I shared his bed. I felt bad about making him sleep on the couch and with Casanova between us, I felt protected. Petru lightly kissed my cheek before we fell asleep. I turned immediately away, but I squeezed his hand to let him know that it was okay. Behind my eyes as they closed, I was waiting for Neela.

The next day, I stayed in the special place I had chosen by the café and the white church. It was close to Petru's square, and the café had good food and coffee for my breaks, though it felt weird to take breaks and sip cappuccinos without a mask. I used my glasses then.

Once the café women realised I was deaf, they wrote little notes:
WHERE ARE YOU FROM?
WHERE DO YOU LIVE IN VENICE?
HOW OLD ARE YOU?
ARE YOU IN SCHOOL?

Their questions were like the ones asked by Indian men who sometimes scribbled to me—HOW YOU LIKE INDIA? But they were also concerned because I was so young and alone. I tried to act older. My seriousness and the mime job helped. I told them I was seventeen like Petru.

ALMOST 18. I wrote.

It made them feel better. I had finished secondary school. I was traveling with friends before going to a university. I loved Venice, such a wonderful city. Lying was easy and people tended to be sympathetic to the deaf. Although I hated it when they thought we were incapable or called us handicapped, I loved to prove them wrong, prove I could do anything at all.

The days passed. I made nearly 60 euros a day sometimes. I paid back Petru and bought more clothes. Underwear. Flowing skirts. Tank tops. I wanted to blend in here. I liked that what was common here was sacrilegious exposure in India. I was a rebel in a rebel city. My arms became strong. Their muscles bulged from being held up for long periods of time. I ran my fingers along them at night. Their strength empowered the rest of me. Lifted me up and gave substance to my body. Though inside: somewhere between my new muscles and bones—I still felt hollow. I smiled with my papier-mâché mask and it became an extension of my own skin. I was paper, too. Glued together. Painted. Golden.

DISCOVERED

It had been over two weeks since the afternoon when I leaped into the canal, away from my new apartment and away from Father. I was in my usual spot, standing to the left of the white church by the café. It was just after my lunch break. I was energised and ready to maintain a difficult position of arms raised high. Branches reaching up towards the balconies above. The sun gleamed brightly upon the gold flecks of my arms and clothes. I saw the red hair first and hoped it was an illusion. Messy curls wildly sticking out from the sides of a tall lanky man's head. Blue-green eyes largely searching the crowds around him.

I stopped breathing. The man paused near the church and sat down on the steps 30 or so feet away from me, eyes turned towards the crowds passing in the street. I couldn't take my eyes off him. He looked skinnier. I could see the round circles of sweat spreading out from beneath his arms, darkening his worn sea green T-shirt. He carried a pad and paper. As I watched, breath still in my throat, he wrote in jerking motions across the pages. His eyes didn't even look down. He didn't want to miss a single face as it passed.

More money fell into my basket. I barely noticed. I hoped I succeeded in becoming a tree completely. A mural painted on the side of the café. Anything but the lost daughter of the man I watched. Prey eyeing its predator. Maybe I could have left as his eyes turned away. But when his sweeping stare arched across the crowds and rested upon me, penetrated into the gold-rimmed holes of my mask, I knew I was discovered.

The fear inside pushed the air out of my mouth quickly. My tree-body began to breathe in gasps that shook my branches. The more I trembled, the deeper he stared. Until, like a shark snapping its tail and taking off, Father dropped his pen and paper, rose up from the step, and bounded over to me before I could run, or move, or lift my hands to hold the flimsy papier-mâché mask to my face.

He grabbed one of my shoulders with one hand while ripping my precious mask off my face with the other. I felt the tearing of the ribbon from the side of the mask like a tearing of my own skin. My hand flew up to the side of my face where the tear would have been. Once my face was bare to him, my flood of tears cracking the gold beneath my eyes, carrying it into tiny rivers of dust down my cheeks and neck, wetting the top of my shirt, he stopped. I read the moan upon his lips as his eyes wept in a way that made me feel ashamed. I couldn't keep their gaze. But once I looked down, he took me roughly in his arms and squeezed the air out of me.

When he finally let me go, he frantically signed: *Why?*

I just looked at him. Felt the people glancing towards us as they passed. Felt my mask and its broken ribbon lying facedown on the street beside me. I wanted to reach down and pick it up, but I couldn't escape Father's eyes. This was the man who stole me from Mother and my country, and ripped me from India, tore me away from my lover. Yet—I was now a tree, an actor, in a city of more joy than I had ever really known. I was someone here, a faceless beautiful tree by a café. I was something people marveled at, painted gold like a temple. And he was the reason for that, too.

When I didn't answer, he got more anxious. He stooped down and grabbed at the money in my basket, then stared at my costume, down at the mask against the pavement, as if it was being punished. A piece of my own face, burrowing in shame. He looked back into my eyes and signed, *What are you doing? Making money, dressing up, having fun while I am searching for you? I've been crazy thinking I lost you!*

I took a deep breath and signed, *I was angry. I left and couldn't find my way back. I needed money for food!*

How did you leave? How was it possible for you to leave from your room? C-a-n-a-l.

You swam? I told you that was unsafe! And where have you been sleeping? With friends. They are safe. They helped me.

They helped a 15-year-old run away from her home. That's not helping. We're going home. Now.

Wait! I have to tell my friend!

No way. You didn't tell me when you left.

I tried to push my way towards the café to give the women a note for Petru. He would be worried. But what could I do? Father had my arm in a grip that would've hurt if I bothered to think about it. I had to grab my mask off the ground fast in order to keep it. It was broken like me. I clasped it to my chest as Father hurried me through the crowded street. I wanted to escape again. Slip away. But some part of me didn't allow the rest to break free. Captured without even a cage. I could do one thing. Since I learned Venice, I knew where we were. I could remember it. Sneak back to Petru.

I realised Father's apartment was in *Cannaregio*, on the side of Venice near the island where they buried their dead, *San Michele*. Behind the Grand Casino that was across the Grand Canal from Petru's apartment. It seemed close, but it really wasn't. I could swim it, but climbing out near Petru's apartment would be hard to do unseen. The streets would have to be the only way. Father did what I knew he would. He led us into the apartment and signed, *You're not shutting this door. You're not going out. You're staying right here until you start school in S-e-p-t-e-m-b-e-r.*

I was tired of fighting and escaping. I walked past the mint rice walls, into my room, found my elephant sheets, and crawled under them.

The next morning I woke early to fabric elephants rather than a real dog's nose. I wanted Casanova. Leaning up, through my wide-open bedroom door, I could see the back of Father's legs where he sat in the kitchen. There was a tattoo of a curling ocean wave behind his left calf that I had never seen. I fished around in my bag for my blue sunglasses. Thankfully, I had had them with me the day before. There were still clothes at Petru's apartment, though. I rose as quietly as I could, and tiptoed over to the balcony. I left the door open, slid down into the black metal chair, heated from the sun. It almost burned the skin on my arms, but I didn't care. I leaned my head against the railing and closed my eyes. At least my cage was pretty. The lapping water below was a small comfort.

I jumped when I felt a splash of water against my bare feet. Opening my eyes, I looked down to see a small two-person kayak floating below me. Sitting on it were Casanova in the front and Petru in the back, paddle in hand, smiling widely. He had a plastic bag in his hands with a long rope tied to it. Pointing down at it, then back at me, I understood that it was my clothes. A note was tied to the string above the bag. He threw the other end of the rope up to me. After one or two tries, I caught it and could pull my bag up to the balcony. Casanova barked. I motioned for him to be quiet, as I hurriedly opened the note and read: NOOLA, it started. The phonetic spelling of my name made me smile. I HOPE YOU ARE OK. I THOUGHT YOUR FATHER FIND YOU. THE WOMEN AT CAFÉ TELL ME THEY SEE YOU LEAVE WITH MAN LIKE YOU WITH RED HAIR. CASANOVA FOLLOW YOUR SCENT. I WAIT AND COME TO WINDOW, BECAUSE I KNOW YOUR FATHER ANGRY. I HOPE YOU ARE NOT ANGRY WITH ME, BUT I MUST LET YOU STAY HERE. I CANNOT KEEP YOU AWAY FROM FAMILY. YOU KNOW WHERE TO FIND ME.

His note brought tears to my eyes behind the glasses. I wanted to jump down into his boat, but I remembered a promise to Mother long ago. To stay with father, to watch over him. I broke it once, but I didn't have it in me to do it again. I nodded my head at Petru, signed, *I'll come see you!*

He smiled and nodded. He waved back and paddled away. As I watched his boat slowly move down the canal, Father came up behind me and grabbed the note. When he finished it, he looked up, still angry, but I started before he could, *See!? He said he can't take me from you! He's on your side! Aren't you happy?*

He stared at me for a while with thoughts I couldn't see moving behind his eyes. Finally he responded, *You're still not going out. You're staying here until I know you won't run away again.*

He handed the note back to me and walked away. I stood there, half in sunlight, half in shadow. Betrayed by them both.

A week passed slowly. I sat on my balcony day after day. Like an old lady, watching the world pass by from behind my large blue-rimmed glasses. My skin became burnt around my shoulders where it wasn't used to so much sunlight. Father tried to give me sunscreen, but I didn't want to use it. It didn't feel natural. Nobody used it in India. But my skin seemed to know by itself what I didn't want to admit—I wasn't exactly Indian. I held the mask often, tracing my fingers over the cracks in the cheek, the torn ribbon. I slept with it in my arms like a doll. Sometimes Petru came to see me on his boat at night. Or he waved from across the canal, Casanova barking from the courtyard in the distance. I smiled every time but I grew cold inside like the deep parts of the water below me.

I was ready to suffocate from the lack of motion and exploration when Father began to let me go walking with him. It was his way of trying to see if he could trust me to live as a normal daughter. A girl that could say: *Dad, can I go get some ice cream? I'll be back early, I promise.* He was as tired of the punishment period as I was. He wrote less. Often he just sat at the other balcony, staring out like me. We must have looked like strangers, occupants of separate apartments.

The crowds might have allowed me to slip away from him, but I didn't. The cracked mask in my handbag held me back like a broken leg. In a courtyard, down on the far eastern end of Venice, we saw a mime I didn't know playing a violin. People clustered around the short girl with the long curling dark hair. Her large breasts were held tight together in a corset that caused them to spill out over the top. I hadn't seen that much cleavage on a woman in public. It embarrassed me, but I couldn't take my eyes off her. The dress she wore was something from the fifteenth or sixteeth century. Blood red crushed velvet. Rose-coloured satin shining in the midday light. Ruffles of cream and black lace. She must have been sweating beneath the layer of fabric. Her face captivated me more than her breasts: a sophisticatedly large nose, a wide smiling mouth, eyes closed to the music, head tilted against the curve of the violin as her arm danced the bow back and forth across it. It reminded me of the famous tune from our area of Ireland: *Pórt Na bPúcaí*, the song of the fairies or the pookas.

An Blascaod Mór, the Great Blasket Island and meeting place of my parents, was a place where people lived years ago. First there were monks living in the hermit huts at the back of the island. Then there were small groups of people who built a village of thirty or so homes near the beach facing the mainland. In the early 1900s, the population swelled to nearly two hundred, but by 1953 the 22 people who were left finally abandoned the island.

Now it was a historical site. Tourists and locals like myself and Mother went there. We locals rode the small ferryboats for free, so we made sure to take advantage of it. It was Mother's home, after all. At five I played in the hermit huts with her. We would hide from Father. I liked the westernmost island, *An Tiaracht*, because it looked like a pointed wizard's hat. Mother said people used to have to fly to it because otherwise they couldn't get a boat near its steep rocks without crashing. She said the anger of the waves and the sea was only above. In its depths, all was calm.

The south side of *An Blascaod Mór* faced another island, *Inis Mhic Uileáin*, where one of the Blasket families had moved. They wanted to try and live out there alone. Their own island. Seals slept there as well. The family brought their animals and their violin. One night, they swore they heard a strange melodious tune the wind had carried into their small cottage. The man began to play his own violin along with it. Everything went quiet except for this sad moving music. They never discovered where it came from, but the man kept playing it. And when they finally gave up the solitude, gave the island back to the seals and the gulls, they kept that tune when they returned to *An Blascaod Mór*, and on to the mainland. *Pórt Na bPúcaí* it became, for its mystery and its beauty.

I used to place my hands upon the violin when Mother played it for me. The vibrations pulsed through my small fingers. It made me cry. Looking back, I understood how the loneliness of such a tune, its singular beauty unlike any other sound, was something my child heart couldn't fathom yet.

It passed through me. A quiver in my bones. A gentle wind turned cold. Unattainable.

Back in the Venetian courtyard, I watched the musical mime. Her eyes opened and looked towards me as I turned my gaze away. Slowly peering back up, I still couldn't meet her eyes. Not close enough to see their colours. Only her breasts. A safer haven. Everyone was staring at them. Glancing up, yes. Even Father.

We moved on. In a bookstore Father signed, *You should read something. I'll buy you a book, ok?*

I guess. I have my own money.

Better for you to save your money. What if you run away again? He turned as he finished, forcing me to search the shelves for something to read.

Finding a book was hard. I didn't know where to start. I had been glancing through my Tamil books during the past few days but they didn't interest me anymore. I browsed through books about Venice. Mermaids. Ships. Gambling. *Carnivale.* Poetry? I hadn't read much of it in English. Mother kept many old Irish poems. She signed them to me until I could read them myself. But I never read the English translations. I didn't see the point of reading something that had been changed in order for other people to understand it.

A blue book with a sketch of a beautiful woman intrigued me. She had a necklace of pearls. Large eyes, perfect straight Italian nose. Small pointed lips. She looked like most women painted by Michelangelo and Leonardo da Vinci, but her eyes had something else. Her entire bust was a sketch in blue tones. Light and dark. Flat book cover. White text: Veronica Franco. *Poems and Selected Letters.* I opened it to see poetry in both Italian and English, facing each other. I could read the translations line by line. A more interesting way to learn some Italian. The back cover: dark blue with tiny white lines arranged in boxes. Veronica Franco: a courtesan. What was a courtesan? She made her living from her beautiful face and body. A prostitute? And a poet? I didn't care about the rest. I handed the book to Father. He didn't look especially pleased when he examined the back cover, but the Italian and the poetry it included must have made it seem okay. I could tell he didn't want to discuss it though. He got it for me. *Thank you.*

Instead of a nod, his head wagged side-to-side. It looked weird coming from him. I didn't like it, so I turned away and tried not to think of Neela, *Ammā*, Mathi. Wagging Indian heads. I hugged my new blue book to my chest as we walked home through the crowds.

WINGS

Veronica Franco—I didn't know she would be able to speak in my own voice, without having known me, having lived so long ago. Her voice reached me through those translated white pages. A recent printing. I couldn't even tell if the English was done well, or what it was missing. Entire concepts were missed in translations from Irish to English. What was missing here? What lay between these dead and living stones, between Veronica's skin and the smooth fabrics of her gowns?

It took another week before Father finally exhausted himself with his own punishment. I had taken to walking around the apartment, reading my poetry book. I pretended it was the 1500s. I wore saris again because they looked more like the old-fashioned dresses than my flowing skirts. I played with them, wrapping myself in all kinds of ways as I tried to mimic the sort of dress Veronica Franco would have worn. Sometimes I tried reading Father's notes. Flipped through his photos of hammerhead sharks, bright yellow and silver fish, porpoises, pink and brown coral reefs. He didn't mind when I looked at his pictures, but the times when I tried to read what he was writing over his shoulder, he shooed me away.

Veronica was smart and strong in the ways I wanted to be. Sometimes, after reading a poem, I would sit and talk to her. My hands and face moved as if she sat right in front of me. Watching. Laughing. Crying with me. I imagined some of her lines to be a direct confession to me, or more—a response. Whoever she loved had not been Neela, but she knew because she took the feeling from my own heart and wrote it out across the page. I tried to sketch Veronica's portrait from the blue cover of my book, but it was yet another thing to hide.

I still couldn't talk to Father. He pored over his notes, travel books from Indonesia, and biology texts. He didn't have friends and we barely communicated with each other. How could he possibly understand what I was going through? He came into my room one day when I was signing to

Veronica. I stopped, but he had already seen. I felt the flush rise up into my cheeks. He just looked at me and signed, *Are you bored? Do you want to do m-i-m-e work again?*

I was caught off-guard. *Of course, I do.* I managed to sign. *You'll let me?*

If you tell me exactly where you're going and you come back when we decide.

Ok! I signed fast before he even finished.

I can't force you to stay here for another month. But do you promise me that if I let you do this, you'll stay here and go to school in the fall?

Yes. Of course! A thousand times: yes.

The weeks of my entrapment were over. I left in a new blue skirt and white tank top. My mask and costume were tucked into my handbag. I went directly to the square where I met Petru. Casanova saw me first. He came bounding towards me and almost knocked me over. His wet paw prints were all over my clothes but I let him lick me until Petru came running over to us.

I was locked in his arms before I could do anything to protest. When he finally let me go, he reached over to gently lift off my sunglasses and stared into my eyes. When his hand began to pet my hair like a dog, I smiled and pushed it away, signing, *What?*

It was one of the only signs he knew. His arms flapped up and down in exasperation as he pointed to me and acted out in gesture that I was alone, no tall father behind me, scolding me, and so on. A few people stopped to watch him as they passed and I laughed. Casanova had given up his excitement and just sat on my foot watching his master's antics with his tongue hanging way out of his mouth.

We went for gelato. Petru claimed that he knew Father would give me a break at some point. I was just excited to be able to go back to my work and wanderings. I took out my Veronica Franco book to show Petru. I was trying to figure out which Italian word meant "wings."

Petru laughed at me and wrote: YOU ARE TRYING TO LEARN ITALIAN FROM AN ENGLISH TRANSLATION OF FIFTEENTH CENTURY LOVE POEMS WRITTEN BY A WHORE! YOU CANNOT EVEN FIGURE OUT THE WORD FOR WINGS!

THEN WHAT IS IT?!

ALI. ONE WING IS ALA. OK?

I looked at him with my eyebrows pushed up together and my eyes narrowed until he apologised, trying to explain that he thought I was making it harder on myself. He did respect Veronica. I wrote about her life until my hand hurt. I quoted my favourite lines in Italian without even looking at the book. They were about rivers standing still and the sea calming its rage because of the tears between Veronica and her lover. I loved using water metaphors for my own emotions, too.

THESE WORDS ARE VERY USEFUL IN ITALIAN!

Petru wrote, YOU WRITE THIS TO PEOPLE, THEY THINK YOU CRAZY!

I wrote more about Veronica's lovers and the harshness of her society towards women.

He looked worried about my sudden passion for her and her story, and finally asked me a question I was not ready to answer: WHAT DO YOU KNOW OF LOVE?

I froze before looking up into his eyes. The very mention of love flooded me with memories. Once again, I felt tangled in dark hair, drowning, alone, apart. Heart entirely missing from my shell of a body. I was a skeleton with skin stretched over it in the shape of a girl. Fallen. Broken. Staring up at Petru, who suddenly stopped laughing. Gazed back with eyes like a seal. Compassion. Comprehension. Serenity. I let myself lean against him. His long arm wrapped around me. A moment later, I had to move away. And then we just walked.

The next day I found another mask. This one was bright blue with black and silver traced along its edges. It perched over my nose, covered only the top half of my face. A dream I had of myself sinking in water, falling towards a submerged Venice on the ocean floor, moved me to want my skin painted blue or grey. A colour of the sea. I started wearing the flowing skirt of my turmeric-coloured half-sari. I dared to wear the similarly coloured sari-top with nothing else. It was hot enough. The exposure of my white stomach made me nervous, but the thought that I could paint it blue like the mask excited me. I could have new skin.

I would try some Indian dancing. Neela and I used to play-dance in our room at night, trying to mimic the movie stars we watched. I didn't know if I was any good, but it was fun. A way for my body to sing to itself. I didn't think it could compare to the dancing of Mother and her selchies. I used the same basket for money and started in the place where I mimed before. While dancing, I accidentally signed the lyrics of the Tamil love songs that Neela used to write down for me. I let the signs flow from one to another as they naturally began to merge with the dance of my arms. My cheeks flushed with embarrassment when groups of people came to watch me. Not all of them put money into my basket but everyone stood by me for a while. The fake smile I used in my dance slowly relaxed itself into something wider and real. I didn't notice Petru and Casanova sitting off to the side near the steps where I had seen Father. Once my eyes met his, I nearly tripped. Instead I let my dance come to a gradual end as quickly as I could gracefully manage, and gathered my things.

Petru rose to meet me with an expression I had never seen on his face before. His eyes were wide and his cheeks flushed.

What? I signed.

He drew large circles around his eyes and mimicked his jaw hanging down, then drew in the air WOW in huge letters. I laughed and bent down to pet Casanova. I couldn't believe how much money I had made in only a short afternoon of dancing. Over a hundred euros.

Petru wrote to me: THIS IS WHY I TOLD YOU BEFORE TO MOVE! YOU ARE WONDERFUL! BUT DON'T GET TOO EXCITED ABOUT THE MONEY —EVERY DAY IT CHANGES—YOU KNOW? AND SUMMER MEANS MANY TOURISTS. NOT MUCH WORK OTHER TIMES.

I know. I signed. I wasn't doing it for the money.

Weeks passed unusually fast. Fleeting conversations with Father. Papers piling up in our apartment. A journal I began to write in. Petru learning more sign. Trips with Petru, Casanova, Gio, and Michel to the beach, *San Michele* (the island of the dead), and *Murano* (the island of glass making and art). Gio's dark eyes on me, whenever I looked up towards him and immediately looked back down. Work in the square. Dancing. Smiling. The top of my hand brushing against Gio's arm, unnecessarily. Money in my basket, then inside a secret drawer, piling up. Savings. Someday—escape.

In the final days of summer, I met Zosia upon her return from a trip back home. My phantom mime from the east of Venice: the violin player. If I had a heart, it would have leaped into my throat when I saw her rush through their apartment one late afternoon. Gown-less yet still brilliant. Wide hips curved beneath her thin dark violet dress. Long curling locks of hair hung down alongside them. Instead of a trembling feeling in my breast, I felt wet in a place I had forgotten.

I could hardly meet her eyes until Petru called her over to me and introduced us. Her smile was so soft that I wanted to climb into her lips and slide through the glossy texture I could feel from three feet away like the flesh of wet tulips. The scent of musk she wore made it difficult for me to breathe. In a flash, she was gone. Having rushed back out as quickly as she entered. Violin in her hands. Carrying a myth and beauty I couldn't handle. I guided the memory and scent of her back into the gown-clad mirage from that courtyard. Made her play *Pórt Na bPúcaí*. A dream. A ghost in passing, moving somewhere else. I didn't want another woman anymore.

A few days before my first day of school Petru told me that he was leaving. We were sitting on his balcony, watching the boats glide past as the sun set.

What? My hands shook as I asked.

He knew more signs. Between signs and mime, he probably could have told me without grabbing a pen. I saw tears in his eyes and his arms looked heavy.

He wrote: I DON'T WANT TO GO. BUT I BEEN HERE SINCE SPRING, AND NOW I MUST GO TO ANOTHER CITY FOR WORK IN WINTER. RAIN COMING, AND THATS BAD FOR STREET WORK. LOCAL MIMES GET WORK DURING LOW SEASON, NOT ME. MY FRIENDS HERE HAVE TOLD ME MANY OTHER PLACES IN SOUTH AND NORTH. MAYBE GREECE. I WILL COME BACK NEXT SUMMER. OK?

I felt stupid, but I cried anyway. I grabbed at Casanova, who licked my tears, but he didn't want to be inside my arms. Petru held me. I felt his heart beating fiercely against the side of my face. The scent of his sweat was faint, salty like the ocean. I was nervous sitting that close. His fingers touched the side of my cheek. Wiping my tears. Tilting my head before I could think about what he might be doing. Lips. Suddenly lips upon lips. Soft, then tongue. I jumped back. The tongue felt gross to me. But his eyes made me lean back into him. This time I clenched my teeth shut so his tongue wouldn't get past. Just tried to kiss him with lips only. He responded and held back. It was better, but it wasn't her. This was Petru, my friend. But he was leaving. How else could I keep him? After kissing me for a few minutes, he stroked me like a doll while Casanova curled at our feet.

The day after Petru left, I walked into the apartment to find Zosia sitting against his bedroom door smoking and crying. I stepped towards her awkwardly, my heart pumping against my chest in irregular beats. She looked at me nonchalantly, waving the hand that held her cigarette before inhaling. I sat down beside her and tried to ask her what was wrong by pushing my eyebrows together. She moved her hand as if she were writing in the air. I reached into my bag and pulled out my pad and pen, purposely touching her fingers with mine as I handed them to her.

She wrote in messy cursive I could barely read: HE WAS SUPPOSED

TO TAKE ME WITH HIM OR STAY HERE WITH ME, BUT HE LEFT WITH HIS SILLY DOG. WE WERE DATING FOR MONTHS BUT I WENT AWAY FOR A FEW WEEKS AND HE STILL CAN'T JUST BE WITH ME – HE HAS TO CHASE EVERY OTHER GIRL HE CAN FIND.

I wrote back hurriedly, completely taken aback by her words: YOU MEAN PETRU? She nodded. HE NEVER TOLD ME YOU WERE DATING!

NO, HE WOULDN'T. HE'S RIDICULOUSLY PERFECT, A SWEETHEART, A GENTLEMAN, BUT HE CAN'T STAY WITH ONE GIRL. HE CRAVES HIS FREEDOM EVER SINCE HE LEFT HIS CONTROLLING FAMILY BACK IN CORSICA. I KNOW HE LIKES YOU, TOO. IT'S FINE. HE HAS NEVER BEEN FAITHFUL. HE LOVES EVERYONE TOO MUCH.

I'M SO SORRY. I DIDN'T KNOW.

I felt like an idiot for not noticing it, but I couldn't remember him ever staring at other girls or talking with them much while he was with me. I was out of words, so I ventured a touch—her arm, just a squeeze, and she crumpled into my lap.

HOME

I didn't know what to do without Petru. Zosia was busy most of the time and I rarely saw her again after the afternoon that she cried in my arms. School began and I hadn't made any friends. It was hard enough communicating in different sign languages with my interpreters. Thankfully one of the interpreters had spent some time in Ireland and was able to help me shift over to Italian Sign Language (called LIS, or *Lingua dei Segni Italiana*) more easily. School was different here. The kids had much more freedom than in South India and often behaved wildly or were lazy. I tried to blend in or at least make some friends, but most people didn't pay attention. They had their own groups. I used ISL with Zosia and Petru because it was my first signed language. I liked using LIS with my interpreters at school but it never felt like a language that belonged to my webbed Irish hands.

Every day I came home to Father in the kitchen or on the balcony writing. He had taken up smoking again but was sure to put his fag out the minute I walked through the door. I still smelled it, though. Sometimes he smoked clove cigarettes and I wished he would give one to me, or continue to smoke while I sat beside him, reading. The scent soothed me. It filled the air around me, gave it substance. I was less lonely.

As autumn continued, thoughts of Mother pressed in on me from all sides. It wasn't just Neela I wanted anymore. It was *her*—the woman I came from, who gave me my webbed fingers and toes. The woman who left me first.

I want to go home. Can we go to Ireland for Christmas break? Please? I told Father one morning, interrupting his far-off gaze out the window.

He shook his head as if confused. His eyebrows pushed upwards and together as if something worried him.

We could stay with your friend Tadhg, right? Just for one week. So I can see Mum.

Another new admission. Mother. He was angry anytime I mentioned her. I still believed he just couldn't see her seal body for what it was—her real skin. I knew he thought she left him and abandoned me. Whenever I talked of meeting her by the ocean, he told me to be quiet. *I don't want to hear that,* he signed. I didn't know how he would react after so long. I waited as he sipped his coffee deliberately. Eyes blank as a shark.

Let me call him. Maybe. Ok?

I leapt to my feet and hugged him before I could stop myself. It was the first time I felt any real affection for him. Touching his skin in this way felt alien. I wasn't supposed to embrace him like this, was I? He held me just as awkwardly. We quickly separated. There was pain somewhere inside his downcast eyes as I moved back to my seat.

I tapped on the table to get his attention. *Thank you,* I signed.

The next few weeks were filled with phone calls to Tadhg. I knew it was him based on the haphazard smile on Father's face every time he held his cell phone to his ear. He would quickly turn so that I couldn't read a trace of a word on his lips. Sometimes I tried to spy on him, but he always caught me. The secrecy piqued my curiosity. I remembered Tadhg as a friendly old man, Father's only close friend in our town. He had dark eyes and hair like Mother. The descendants of selchies were known for those traits, but I never asked him about it. I knew that not everyone believed in the myths.

Tadhg was a fisherman who used to run the ferryboat to *An Blascaod Mór*. He was a bit older than my parents. Father told me that his wife had died young and left him with no children. I thought that explained his amicable distance from me. I saw how happy he made Father, and I felt no desire to be close to a man who smelled so strongly of tobacco and whiskey. However, my desire to see Mother cast this old friend in glowing light, a lighthouse where we could take refuge. I had never been to his home, but I imagined it had a guest room with twin beds on opposite walls, tight quarters to bear with Father, but sufferable.

It took weeks for me to get the answer I was looking for: *Tadhg said it was ok. We can go during winter break. Happy?*

I nodded my head while signing *Yes*.

IRELAND

Me: swimming naked in the sea, hair fanning out.

Neela: an eel wrapping around me, sliding up, sliding in.

My mother: a dark shadow down below, in the forest of
long grass.

Me: trying to keep her round form in sight, the grey
between the green.

Waves: pulling water (and me, and Neela) upwards,
towards wind, towards rain.

SAME SKIN

We arrived in Shannon and rented a car to drive out to *Dún Chaoin*, the westernmost edge of Europe. *Na Blascaodaí*. I couldn't wait to be in the *Ghaeltacht*, the Irish speaking areas of Ireland, where I could read the street and store signs in my first language. It cast a different energy over the land, translating it to me. I had forgotten the power of old language closer to the Earth. In the Irish on the road signs, I could smell the grass, wet stones, dirt. As if the Earth itself crowded up between the letters.

The Connor Pass was still there: a narrow winding road through the mountains past Mount Brandon, the second highest mountain of Ireland. The fog wrapped around our small car as we drove slowly through the barren rocky landscapes. As we climbed, I glanced back at the green hills we were leaving and saw the sea. In the distance it looked calm, wide, blue. Brandon Bay was like that. I thought of it as deceptive—the ocean taking on the role of a lake.

As we drove over the top of the pass and headed down, I saw more familiar patches of green beneath the fog. Farther in the distance was Dingle Bay. My favourite trees arched over the sides of the road, all of them leaning to the left, in the direction of the path of wind blowing from the sea. How far the sea stretched, even over land. Past *An Daingean*, past the abandoned stone house where I played as a child. I had pretended I lived there between Dingle Bay and *Dún Chaoin*, surrounded by the steep fields of grazing sheep.

Our car drove over the hill and down towards my home. Finally I could see in the distance: *Na hOileáin. Na Blascaodaí. An fharraige.* I could feel it churning against the cliffs. As we drove down the steep narrow street, barely wide enough for one car, I felt the spell of *Na hOileáin* take hold once again. I was crying. And there it was: *An Fear Marbh*. Sleeping in the sea, oblivious of the waves or perhaps dreaming. *Tar anseo*, I felt it say. As if the words were written on the waves, carried by the wind. My own Irish coming back to me. The language I knew didn't exist without her: Mother, *an bhrúch.*

Ca bhfuil tú, a mháthair?	*Where are you, my mother?*
Abair liom.	*Tell me.*
Cé chomh fada is atá tú uaim?	*How far are you from me?*
Tá mé idir eatarthu. Tá tuirse orm.	*I am in between. I am tired.*
Gan tusa.	*Without you.*
A Mháthair.	*Mother.*
Tá tú san fharraige, sna tonnta.	*You are in the sea, in the waves.*

I felt Father's eyes on the water. Searching for her, too. When I saw the old schoolhouse by the sea in the distance, I remembered the man who raped me. I was down on the rocks close to the water's edge, but I was looking up towards the stone walls of the school when he attacked me. It hurt to see it again, but my yearnings for Mother overpowered the memory of such violence. Maybe Kali had killed him after all.

We reached Tadhg's tiny stone house late in the afternoon. He looked the same to me as always. His huge frame towered over both Father and me. He wore a bulky cream-coloured woolen jumper over dirty brown work pants. His dark beard was longer and his bushy short hair just as disheveled as always. His deep eyes still looked towards the sea, as if he, too, had lost something there long ago. Like most homes on the hillsides of *Dún Chaoin*, his had a spectacular view of *Na nOileán*. The two men greeted each other with a tight embrace and a gaze that could only be interpreted as sadness. We quickly brought our bags inside but the guest room I imagined was not there. Tadhg's home was much smaller than I remembered and he directed me to his couch and Father to a sleeping bag on the floor. I was too excited to be home to care anymore. I grabbed Father's arm and signed, *Mother.*

He nodded with obvious pain in his eyes. Father spoke briefly to Tadhg before we drove off to the place where we saw her most—*Tráigh a' Choma*, our beach. The sun was setting behind *An Fear Marbh* as we drove along the coast. A single boat was sailing through the golden path the sun made along the water. I wanted to be on that boat. Sailing off to her. *A Mháthair. Ar na tonnta.* An old truck was parked in the lot, but the beach seemed deserted. The tide was out and the sea was strangely calm, so we were able to walk down to the place where Father last saw her. The far end where she used to dance.

In the distance, a man stood between the boulders. He was gazing at the sea. I walked closer to Father and let him put his arm around me.

Suddenly he jumped and I thought I heard something loud. Father grabbed my hand and ran towards the sound. I felt Father's panic as if it was coursing through my body rather than his. When we passed around the largest of the boulders, we saw what appeared to be a rifle in the stranger's hands. A large fat body lay at his feet. It bled black liquid into the sand, flowing in small rivers to the place where the waves slapped against the shore. I felt Father's hand let go as he ran faster than I had ever seen. The man gasped as Father knocked him to the ground. Father punched him once and gesticulated towards the body repeatedly. He must have been speaking. I imagined Father saying, *Is brúch í!*

I slowed to a walk. I wanted to reach down and cradle the bloody form at my feet but I couldn't move. *A Mháthair?* I noticed the seal-killer register what Father must have said. He crumbled, too. He flung his gun aside. His hands suddenly in prayer. Bad luck, he knew, to kill a *brúch*. He would never catch another fish nor kill a seal again. I could see through the watery film over my eyes that he too knew the old stories.

Father rushed over and did what I could not. He took the seal's body in his arms. It was the size of me if I had been shortened and filled with blubber. Father lowered his face to hers. *Mo mháthair?* Was it really her? Father's face was covered in her blood. He didn't even seem to notice. He rocked her body, held on so tight that I couldn't watch. I leaned down against her feet. Pressed my fingers into the webs. The webs she gave me. Hers. Mine. Same skin. Wasn't it? I don't know how long we stayed that way. The man disappeared into the night. Seal blood dried on our faces. Our hands were sticky with it. Tangled. Still unable to let go.

Time skipped.

One moment: our bodies wrapped around a seal, covered in its blood.

Next moment: the tide.

We should have known that even though Death creates a great space—a wide gap in the Universe. Place of stillness. Everything else—gone. Despite Death, the sea could move. It could enter that space. It could reach in and take back the body we had stolen. I felt the waves against my legs. Dissolving the blood that still looked black like the sky above us. Was it black? I didn't know. I had never seen seal blood before. The waves crashed harder. Cold. The water was always cold here, though I didn't feel it. My own blood seemed to lower its temperature to match the sea. A twisted kind of harmony.

I knew we had to leave before the tide rushed in, swallowing us with the sand and Mother's body. I didn't want to any more than he did: Father whose head still hung down. It looked like he was sleeping with her. Sleeping with a seal on the beach. It would have been romantic if she wasn't bleeding so much. If she wasn't dead.

I reached out across the wide back of her. It seemed my hand had crossed a mile before it reached his shoulder. I shook until he looked up. Blood clotted over one of his eyes. He had to squint to see me in the dark. I tried signing anyway. *Waves are coming. We have to go, or we'll drown.* I meant him. He would drown. I didn't think I could.

He looked back with no expression on his face. Frozen in sorrow. His sorrow was huge. A monster. It held us, filled us, made us heavy like the boulders along the sand that never moved. No matter how hard the waves crashed against them. Would we stay like that, too? Even when the waves moved up and over our heads? The waves were faster than we could ever be. They would cover us. I knew it. It was the only sensation that forced me to rise. My legs cracked as if they were made of stone, like the Venetian statues, and suddenly I was willing them to move. Pain and tingles shot up my thighs and through my torso, but still—I moved. I leaned across the silky dark body. Even in death, she was so soft. I pulled at him. *A athair,* I thought, *raghaimíd. Más é do thoil é.* He held tighter. The water was now covering half of her body. It had already crashed against him. He was wet. The blood ran down his face in rivers. Down his arms. Collecting in the pockets and crevices of his jeans. I could have stood there forever. Watching the sea take away my parents. No. I couldn't allow it. But could I really do anything? *Father, let's go. Please.*

The waves arrived, pulling at them both. He struggled to hang on to her huge seal body that lay like a soft rock. I reached down and pulled as hard as I could. I kicked him. I screamed. I felt my mouth open and something vibrate in my throat. This made him finally look up at me. See that I was still there, alive. *A athair, táimse anseo.* He tried to speak. I could tell by his mouth moving. I didn't need him to sign it. I knew what he was trying to convey. *We have to bring her. We can't leave her here!* But we both knew how much she weighed. We couldn't drag her. Not with sorrow hanging over us. Filling us like lead. Our gaze locked. Wordless, untranslatable thoughts passed back and forth. We moved. We tried to rush back down the beach, but sorrow held us back. Our hands had met over Mother's face. Her small nose. Her whiskers. My hands burned.

We waded through the crashing waves, half-swimming, down the stretch of disappearing sand, around the unfeeling boulders standing high. This is where Time skipped again. My next feeling was the inside of my sleeping bag, flannel and puffy against my skin, all around me like the blubber of a seal. Pillow against my head. Father on the floor beside me.

I don't remember how many days passed with us at Tadhg's. I know we didn't eat. I felt my stomach rumble more than once. All I saw of Father was the fiery red of his curls escaping from the top of his sleeping bag. Rebelling against the body that wouldn't move anymore. Tadhg spoke briefly to Father after we returned and he retreated to his kitchen and bedroom.

It was early morning when I left the house for the first time. I don't remember doing it. Suddenly I was there again in that space where she died. The tide was low. Tiny waves tumbled over each other, barely able to lift themselves up. Was it because the sea had swallowed Death and now the Sorrow made it heavy? Unable to move anymore? *Tá an fharraige ciúin.*

There was no more blood on the sand. Even the body—her body— was gone. Who had taken it? Was it the sea? Or men? I hoped it was the sea. I sat right in the middle of the Shadow of Death. The Shadow Death made. It would stay for a long time. It was sticky the way seaweed would cling to the rocks and my hands when they were salty. I cried into the sand. My face felt heavy. I pressed it into the grains. Tiny fragments of shells scratched my skin and suffocated my breathing, but I could stay that way for a while. I wanted to be swallowed. Buried among broken shells, between the boulders on this beach. Gone.

Everything was dark. I had to lift my head slightly so that air could reach my gasping lungs. I realised that I wasn't alone. A seal was pushing its way towards me. I had never been close to any others like Mother since that night of summer solstice so many years ago. Had it been only six years? Six felt like twenty. I watched the outline of the seal as it moved. So much like her. I didn't want to see it. Didn't want to be close to one so similar. I looked away until the seal was so near that I could reach my hand out and touch it. The seal's body opened at the top of its head and another head of dark wavy hair pushed out. Her fingers grasped the opening and made it larger as the rest of her face and shoulders followed. Her hair was so long it covered her face and the top half of her body.

I thought I must have been hallucinating. It made me so angry I began punching this thing before me. I hit her arms, her head, her chest where the seal's face stretched across. My throat vibrated as I screamed. Why was I imagining this fake thing that felt like *her*—*mo mháthair, mo mháthair?* She was dead and I hated this thing that stole her form. Whatever Shadow it was, whatever demon. Was it the demon Nīlī? Had she come to eat me like Neela told me?

I hit her until she stopped me. The demon held me in her arms while I continued to scream. I bashed my forehead against her shoulder again and again. Until she pushed me away and her hands moved, *Fionnuala? I didn't die. The seal body you saw here wasn't me. I'm very sad because it was my brother. Your uncle that you met a long time ago. I was on the island and I couldn't get here fast enough. I felt you near but I didn't know for sure.*

She was crying. Her hands were stroking me. I couldn't move for the shock of it all. Couldn't process. Could she be a demon?

Where's your father? She asked.

Tadhg's house. It was all I could sign and I could barely sign that.

She took me up in her arms again. I felt her body where I had hit her. Slowly, regret from those wild punches made me believe she was real—alive. I raveled her wet locks of hair around my fingers like I used to do as a child. Held onto them as she held me. I cried again. Eventually we both relaxed. Leaned back. It was *her* after all. It was really *her*.

What happened to you? She signed more easily. The natural motion of words in her hands was coming back to her after all those years. Her face somehow getting harder or maybe it was the light of the moon.

I didn't know how to respond. She seemed to sense things, but what or how I didn't know. *How much do you know?*

I know you went to India with your father, right?

Yes. Father left me with an Indian family. He went off to work for three years and came back for me. Now we live in V-e-n-i-c-e.

Everything I wanted to tell her before seemed to filter down into the sand. I began to feel afraid that she wouldn't understand any of it. The animal inside me prickled at her eyes staring deeper and deeper, learning things without my words to explain, stealing my secrets before I could even tell her why.

What happened in India? I had never seen her this way: accusing. Sometimes she had this expression with Father, but never to me—never to me.

What do you mean?

I sense something unnatural.

I loved a girl in India and was torn from her like I was torn from you. It was awful but not unnatural. The words fumbled from my fingers, teacups dropping, shattering on a tiled floor. I knew I shouldn't have said anything. I didn't have time to take my words back. Mother picked them up like deformed objects rather than broken ones. *I'm broken, Mummy! Not wrong!* But she couldn't hear my pleas.

You loved a girl like a girl loves a boy?

Yes. You don't understand?

Our words flashed too quickly before my eyes. I couldn't process what she was learning and I couldn't explain it. I knew I had said it *wrong*. I was *wrong* like she thought. I kept remembering that man. Hadn't he made me this way? Was it because every man reminded me of him? I wanted to tell her, the words, they were there on the tips of my fingers, but something kept me from spelling them. My rape shouldn't matter, though, should it? She should love me anyway but she was already slowly moving back to the sea. Recoiling from me? Leaving me without waiting to hear *why*? But I didn't know *why* besides having been raped by a man. I had never planned to love Neela, *a girl*, someone so hard to love, so against what everyone thought was *right*.

How can I understand? In the ocean we have sex in order to give birth. There is no birth from your union. It's not natural. I don't understand. I thought you were like me. I thought you were close with animals—

I had to interrupt her. There were so many questions that she could answer for me, help me to understand: *Wait. Yes I am! I can swim underwater with no air for a long time. My nose can close like your seal nose. My body isn't cold when I'm in cold water. I am like you!* I was losing her. Losing sense of the words rushing through my mind: mymotherhatesme. Shehatesme. Shedoesn'tunderstandwhoIam. WhatamIwithouther? Ican'tbreathe. She's takingmywords, swallowingthem, a monster of the deep, stealingmyability to convey how much I love her, want to be likeherwithherinherthesea.

Then how do you feel these things? I don't believe you. You cut your connection to animals and nature and me. She signed fiercely. Sharp movements in the air. *This is awful! You were so different before. Now I can't even see you.* Her fingernails were the tips of knives, cutting my skin, tiny slashes I could feel stinging me everywhere.

I felt myself disappearing. Not here on this rock. She shredded my gifts and all the qualities of *me* that I valued. Did I deserve this? I knew loving another girl wasn't supposed to be natural. I *had* read about other gay animals in school, though. And what was natural about humans? We wear clothes, walk on paved roads, eat with forks instead of with hands, take pills when we feel any physical pains. She once did these things! She was human too! Wasn't she human anymore?

Mother stared at me wide-eyed and furious, but I felt her inner eyes closing, her light dissolving with a snap of wind. A wall rising up behind her eyes like a tidal made of stone. She stared at me for a long time. Waves stopped rolling. Gulls sat down, stilled, along the edges of the land. Sheep stood still in the long grass. The mouths of cows stopped chewing, blades of green sticking out from their lips. I felt like those blades as I sat before Mother, as if my body were half-devoured in her mouth.

Breaking the spell, she signed sloppily as she continued to inch backwards, and pulled her seal skin up around her body, her eyes turning blacker with each word cast like a spell into the wind: *You're your father's daughter now. I've lost you to humans. I can't live outside the sea anymore. I can't take this form. It feels dirty. I'm sorry. If I raised you, if you stayed here, things would have been different. I wish I had tried harder. I wish I stayed with you.*

I was lost. Her awful incantations caused discord around us: waves crashed, gulls screamed with their wings in frantic flight as if they knew how to sign, sheep ran smashing their fluffy bodies into each other, the cows swallowed their green with foaming mouths crunching sideways as Mother crushed my body in her teeth.

Mum, wait. What are you saying? You're not letting yourself be human anymore? What about seeing father and me? I had to say anything to keep her now. I began to reel all of the ways I could change like a film behind my eyes: nogirls justanimal nohuman nosex nocursing howextremecouldIbe whatelsecouldIdo bethesea likeher becomeaseal.

No. With one sign, one short motion of her right hand, fingers coming together, she cut the film and I felt my dreams unravel into useless ribbons at my feet. *You can tell him that I'm ok but I will never see him again. I'll never forgive him for letting you ruin yourself.*

Correction: *a mháthair,* you have ruined me now. I felt myself crumble, my body bruising like hers. The perfect white skin of her cheek had begun to turn blue like her beloved sea. I reveled in the sight. Wanted to hit her again. Twist her fingers apart so that she couldn't sign this way to me again. Instead of acting out my rage, my hands were messengers from another part of my brain that I wasn't even aware of until I watched their weak pleading: *But I'm not ruined and he's different now. He wants to see you again. He loves you.*

He loves you? I thought to myself. Did I really say that?

Why hasn't he tried to see me for so many years? He left me long ago. We're finished now. I must go back to the sea. I can't stay like this. Without waiting for me, she pulled her seal skin back up over her head, covering all the bruises I gave her. So fast. She was a seal again. Staring out with the same brown watery eyes. Staring for a moment before she turned and flopped towards the sea. I reached out and touched her feet as she left. Their webs. Her skin against my skin. Same skin. Right? Wasn't I still from her? Part of her and the sea? Or was the sea rejecting me, too?

I lay down in the sand. A wish rose in me that I knew was evil but I let it pass through. I wished she had died. Just for a moment. I wished that we had never spoken that way to each other. That she remembered me as *part of her*, as something she could love and understand. I didn't come back to have that change. No. No, I didn't. I didn't come back to have everything freeze within that stone wall behind her eyes.

SPILLING OUT

I knew I shouldn't have told him. I should have known Father wasn't a man of land. His instincts had led him to move his daughter to fish islands floating in a polluted sea. His inclination was to sit daily on his balcony like a sailor staring out. Loving anything water. Our apartment was like a ship quarters to him, I realised. He must have known about Venice: that it was afloat, that it wasn't land. He had no other choice.

When I returned to Tadhg's house to find Father alone, my hands acted as messengers of my newly bruised heart. They relayed their story of how I began to hate myself, how I lost her for both of us, how it was all my fault. He was staring at me with one eye peeking out from the top of his sleeping bag. His body became very still. A predator before striking. Or a man in shock.

He unzipped himself out of his fluffy green sleeping bag slowly. He was crawling as if out of his *skin*. As he lifted his body off the floor, the roll of green looked limp and lifeless. Death's seaweed touch held the green fabric of what had been Father's outer skin in clusters and folds, stuck together and twisted, while he suddenly walked around the room with new purpose. He pushed knives and other tools into the pockets of his jeans. He only wore sturdy fisherman's jeans with so many pockets they could fit anything inside them—a sandwich, a water bottle, dead fish, ropes.

I should have stopped him, but all I could do was stand there— immobile—wishing he would hold me. Tell me I was okay. That I wasn't ruined. It wasn't my fault. I shouldn't hate myself. That he understood. Finally, he said, *I'll be back as soon as possible. I must find her. I love you. Stay here and wait for me.*

What? He was raving mad, but I knew that. I tried to interrupt his sloppy words but he kissed me and went out the door before I could lift my hands from the sides of my body where they hung. *Fuck*, I swore in my head. *Fuckfuckfuck.* I moved over to the floor and climbed into the old green skin he left behind. Still warm. It had a musky odor of sweat and salt and stale breath. Death's sticky seaweed touch covered me, but it felt like Father. Soon, I was asleep.

I woke suddenly. I had slept until the following day. Stomach gave up rumbling. I felt weaker. It was so easy to stay here inside, but something felt wrong. The air was too still. The dream—too real. I drowned. Swallowed the entire sea. *Where was he? A athair?*

I dragged my inner body out of its new skin. The sleeping bag was green like some parts of the sea. *Farraige.* As I crossed the room to the window overlooking the water, I saw what was wrong. *Stoirm.* The grey clouds in the distance were moving quickly over the sea towards me. A cold wind blew in through the window. I realised Father had probably taken a boat out into those swelling waves.

The ocean must not have wanted him to find her. It rose like a champion stretching out, able to expand or detract in size like nothing human. Its mouth could be the size of *An Blascaod Mór.* A monstrous sea. A sea monster. The wind tore at my hair as I ran through the fields, scattering flocks of frightened sheep. I cut through the air despite the pulling I felt along my scalp. My stomach cramped from the hunk of soda bread I had eaten in a rush before leaving Tadhg's. The bread nourished me, but it also reminded my body of how long it had been since I had eaten. A hole freshly opened, stomach expanded, only to find that it was still mostly empty.

I ignored my hunger as I rushed down the narrow road leading to the beach. Even in the mouth of this monster, I could swim better than Father. By the time I reached the place at the foot of the cliffs where the road dissolved into the beach, the sand had disappeared. Instead the waves crashed against the road, lips of the monster, as if they could swallow the road and the cliffs. I couldn't find Father's boat. I thought it must not be far from here, but all I could see were the white-capped peaks of the ocean bursting, rushing, lifting, and deep grey above. *Na hOileáin* looked like the long black gondolas of Venice. But they didn't move.

I leaped down off the farthest rock. *An fharraige, na tonnta.* The water felt cold at first, but my skin absorbed it before it could flood my insides and freeze. My skin, however thin, kept me warm. A shield most humans didn't have. Proving I wasn't just human. I was something else, something like Mother. I dove down deep. As I passed over the long grass swaying down below me, I thought Mother would tie me up like in my dream the night before. I couldn't look at the grass. The surface above was where I needed to focus. I would find him. He would not drown. I grasped the water with my fingers spread wide, and pushed onward.

After a while, I had to breathe. When I breached the surface, squinting through the pouring rain, I had already passed *Inis Mhic Uileáin*, the island of *Pórt Na bPúcaí*, where the seals lived. I didn't know where they went in a storm. I hadn't seen any. I rode waves for a few minutes before diving back down and swimming farther out: towards the rough points of *Sceilig Mhichíl* and *Sceilig Bheag* on the horizon like little hats bobbing haphazardly on the water. The surface above kept its constant motion, continuously spotted with hard rain. Off to my left, I saw dark forms near the top of the water. Moving up and down. I swam closer, trying to determine if they were something to be avoided.

Two forms materialised as the distance between us closed in: it was him. *Athair*. I gasped and choked on a mouthful of water. Father's body was limp like a doll filled with water. It kept sinking down beneath the waves and the other form would push it back up to the air and rain. A dolphin? No. Too round. No dorsal fin above. Could only be—

As I got closer and saw the problem, I felt her. *Máthair*. My skin hummed at the nearness of my parents together, but Father didn't know it. He looked unconscious, maybe even dead. I didn't know how long this had been going on. The sinking. Rising. Sinking. Rising. He didn't even appear to be breathing when he was against the air. I moved up and down with the motion of them, watching as I swam closer. She was trying to keep him afloat but his body, being so limp, couldn't hold onto her. There wasn't enough time to let her save him on her own. I knew she wouldn't succeed.

I dove at him. I could wrap my long human arms around his body, lift him up, and swim. I couldn't look at her, but I felt the jolt run through her seal body when she realised I had swam all this way and was still able to lift him. I pulled him back towards the beach that was gone. Pride gave me added strength. She pushed up beside me and helped me keep him above water. I struggled in spite of my new burst of energy. Neither of us could have done it alone.

The waves thrashed high into the air, smashing against each other in a shower of icy white, and sinking down only to thrash again. The ocean seemed unable to decide what direction to move. Each wave was a liquid animal: breathing, sucking, pushing, lashing. I knew we would drown, but with the abandon of the mad, giving in to the animal inside, the animal outside, those shape-shifting waves, I pressed onwards. The land was there along the edge of my vision. Even when the fog descended and covered it completely, a string tied me to it, pulling me home. I could keep swimming straight ahead.

As quickly as it came, the storm began to falter. My arms began to swallow water, too. Doll arms. I could barely hold onto my parents anymore. My hands slipped off Mother's skin. Father and I plunged into the water. I pulled us up only for us to plunge back in, then up again. The sea was winning, proving itself as Mother's new lover. Mother who probably wanted us to die anyway.

I reviled her. I loathed myself for having told her about my life. In that doubled rage, I pushed and pushed. Half-dragging him off her. But he was too heavy. We had to stay. We had to use Mother for support. Even though the rain eased and the waves subsided, I was exhausted. I wished I had eaten that entire loaf of bread. I felt as if I were filled with water, the sea monster's own liquid fury. Water everywhere, spilling out.

The waves slammed us against the rocks. I couldn't remember the last part of the journey. Just landing. We needed to move fast. Mother pushed us up from below. I climbed and dragged his limp body. The rocks cut my hands and I could feel them start to bleed. I knew Father's skin must have been cut, too, but we had to move faster. The waves chased us up the cliffs.

When we reached the road that curved away from the beach, I pulled Father over to the edge and looked back. Mother sat on the rocks below, looking up at me. She began to bark. I had never seen her bark before, but I knew it from the way she arched her face and opened her mouth again and again. I turned back to Father and started shaking him. I pumped his chest with the little strength I had left in my arms, and breathed into his mouth again and again. Nothing. He was soaked and there were tiny red scratches on his cheeks and nose. His face was swollen with its skin nearly blue. But I kept trying. I saw Mother waiting out of the corner of my eyes, but I didn't wait to see whether she was still barking or not.

Just when I couldn't keep pumping, couldn't even breathe, he started to choke. I turned his head to the side as water spewed out of his mouth. He was alive. As soon as he saw her down below, he reached out his hand. She was still barking when she looked at me. I couldn't tell if it was tears or the rain in her eyes. I tried to will her to change. Break out of her seal skin again. Embrace us. Forgive us. Her eyes traveled from his outreached hand to his half-closed eyes to me. She nodded before turning and flopping back down into the surf below.

Agus d'imigh sí as radharc.   *And she vanished completely.*

What was there in her eyes before she left? Nothing I was able to see clearly. I couldn't tell if she was proud of me, but I hoped maybe a little. I pulled Father into me, held him like a child. His face buried itself into my chest for the first time and his outstretched hand brought itself around me. In the past, if I had been given a choice between them, between Father and mother, I would never have chosen him. Now, I didn't know. I was half-animal, but less animal than her. How could I question her? Seal or selchie, she was a part of the sea in a way that I would never be. Still, something in her felt too bitter. Frozen in a way I didn't want to be.

I held Father tight. The wind and the rain had chilled me to the bone. Bones wrapped in too-thin layers of skin. Empty hole in my stomach. Hollow cavernous heart as it let the water spill out.

I held him tight. Because a part of me was rejecting her. Letting her disappear. Letting her be a seal if she couldn't bear to be human.

I held him because I hadn't chosen him. But from the way he didn't look back at the sea when she left, the way he raised us up and began our walk up the road, and the way he supported my doll-body with his own barely-enlivened one, he had finally chosen me.

When we returned to Tadhg's house, he sat us down in his kitchen with brown bread and soup. Tadhg looked straight into my eyes and began telling a story for the first time since I had known him. Father translated:

I met my wife on the beach. She was naked. She was a s-e-l-c-h-i-e. My family told me the story of the seal people for many years. Long ago, my grandfather married a seal woman, too. Now it was my turn. She was beautiful. She had long dark hair like your mother. I became friends with your father when I saw who he married. I knew that he would have great sorrow. I'm sorry I was never close to you and that I never signed. I have a problem. I can't make children. So when my wife left me, she left me with nothing. When I see you, when I spent time watching you grow, I feel more sorrow. It's too hard to try and communicate with you. Too hard to be near you because I am so sad. My wife is gone and I have nothing. You're lucky to have your father, and he is lucky to have you. Do you understand?

I sat with my hands on the table for a long time. Tears flowed down my cheeks, but I couldn't find any words inside myself to give back to Tadhg. Not yet. But I knew I had at least one more ally, one more person to call a friend, an elder who was part of my family's legend, too. Tadhg had proven to me that Father and I hadn't simply shared a delusion. Mother really was a selchie, and there were others out there, too.

I T A L Y

Wine: in dark bottles, promising stained tongues.

Rolling papers: wrapping leaves ready to be burned.

Mountains: rising out of the land, green cutting itself into
the sky.

Clocks: ticking away, every second closer to discovery,
punishment, death.

Hands: with webs, opening, telling tales, dreaming their
way towards connection, forgiveness.

RUPTURES

On a Friday night I sat on the balcony of Gio and Zosia's apartment, looking at the still half-finished casino across the canal, when Gio passed me his pipe and lighter. I knew he smoked some sort of drug, but Petru wouldn't talk to me about it. Usually Gio didn't do it in front of me either.

Father and I had returned to Venice weeks before but neither of us were able to talk about what happened back in Ireland. We also couldn't talk about anything else. I roamed the streets when I wasn't in school, visited with Zosia, watched the mimes and street performers preparing for Carnivale. Gio was always there. I think he noticed something different in me since I got back. I watched him sometimes, wondering what he thought about, who he loved, if he had ever been betrayed.

My hands reached out as if it were something natural. Clicked the lighter. My mouth inhaled as if it was taking a normal breath of air. Only it was warmer. A cloud melted into me so that I felt smoky, too. My body was suddenly light. My arm floated on the wind as it reached out to Gio and handed back his pipe. A smile spread across my face as I looked at him. Drawn to the shape of him sitting next to me. My eyes moved on to follow the edges of the black railings. I shivered when I touched them, and Gio put his arm around me. Hard muscles, squeezing me like Petru never would.

Gio was a man, though. A man who was touching me. Flashes of that other man passed before my eyes. I was trembling inside because of the memory and the fear but I knew with marijuana, or what we called *ganja* in India, I needed to focus on positive things, rather than negative ones. I didn't want to start freaking out. And Gio was just a boy, really. Not the kind of man who raped or abused. Right? The railings were breathing, too. I watched them move in and out, imprisoned by those narrow black bars and Gio's arm locked around my shoulders. I wanted to stop fearing men. In the skin of Gio's arm, I wanted more healing beyond what Neela tried to do for me. Flowers across the canal: barely discernible dots of blue that grew large and small again. Everything was breathing. Everything telling me to relax.

I didn't realise that I had become numb until Gio's face came close to me, and his lips pressed against mine. Where was the pipe? I tried to look for it, but he held me there. His breath was heavy in my mouth. Heavy like his hands on my arms, my back. His body leaned towards me, pushed me backward and pulled me up. Guided me to his room on the other side of the apartment. Across the living area, we tripped and fell onto the couch. Groping hands lifted me up and I felt like I was floating. My body stretched into air and I was spread out onto his bed. I liked the soft mattress beneath me. It countered the hard boy above me. What could we do here? Anything.

The room itself quivered like the part of Gio that pushed against my stomach as he kept kissing my lips, my cheeks, ears. It tickled, but the tickle itself seemed to affect me in soft waves. I trembled. Wait—was that my skin, spreading more, peeling off? Bra pushed up around my neck like its own red roll of flesh. His face on my breasts, but I couldn't feel it. Pulsing air. The air itself seemed made of transparent bugs all moving and climbing over each other. I watched it as he peeled my cloth-skin down to my ankles and suddenly his hands were softer. Circling me where I grew wet without meaning to, trembling from his warm breath, his lips against me.

His hands ripped at something. Material I felt through my skin, through his skin, down to the stretchy thing he rolled onto himself before I could try and think about what we were doing, or how late, or Father, or how Gio opened me and pushed his body inside. The rest of him lay down across the rest of me. Lips against my lips again. Potent scent of smoke and sweat. Salty. Thick. His tongue across my mouth as his hips pushed against mine. I moved in and out of our joined flesh. Up and down. Sometimes into the mattress, sometime high against the ceiling. Until—was he screaming? Eyes closed, mouth open. Liquids moving, rushing, spilling, filling something inside. Then fast pulling out, plastic cold against my skin.

I wanted to roll into the covers of his sheets and roll away. He handed me a glass of water and I saw the clock glaring in vibrant green letters 1:47. I had to go. Father would be angry. Go home. Where was home? Where was the rest of me? Scattered on this floor? Pieces of me. All apart. Wet. Cold.

Naked Gio helped put me back together again like a doll. I climbed back into my costume. Zosia was walking past Gio's bedroom as I opened the door and our bodies banged against each other. All three of us stopped and looked at each other in the dark. I felt Zosia's concern as she eyed my disheveled body and Gio's naked chest behind me. Suddenly she pushed me out of the way and ran at Gio, slapping his arm and yelling. All I saw on her lips was the word *you*. He shouted back, his face contorting into something monstrous and ugly. I stood by the front door of the apartment, wondering if I should slip out.

I didn't want Zosia to ruin this. Ruin the high I felt and the way Gio must have healed me because I was not afraid anymore. I knew what men were now. Before I could make my move, Gio turned around and slammed his bedroom door. Zosia turned to me, grabbed my still-numb arm, and led me into her room.

I slid down onto the edge of her bed covered with dark satin sheets. She switched on a low lamp and searched for a pad and paper. Without even looking at me, she started writing: I DON'T KNOW HOW THAT BASTARD GOT YOU INTO HIS BED! YOU LOOK HIGH—ARE YOU OK? DID HE FORCE YOU? I'M SORRY I GOT IN LATE AND DIDN'T REALISE YOU WERE HERE!

The room began to spin. Painted blue walls revolved around my thoughts of Gio's body, mine, the rocks along the Irish coast, blood on the rocks, my hands, scraping. I covered my face with my hands and cried into the deep purple satin fabric around me. I had tried. I had tried to use Gio to heal, but the kindling of the memories from Zosia's words *did he force you* brought too much back up to the surface, playing it like a movie before my eyes. This time she held me.

The next day I couldn't look at Father. Felt blush rising in my cheeks as I tiptoed past him at the kitchen table. Writing. He never did anything else. Except fish out on the edge of the islands, or watch boats passing in the canals. Hot coffee waited on the counter. I don't think Father ever turned it off, even to sleep. Such a peculiar waste of power. I poured it into a black mug, left its inside black, too. Retreated back to my room. One wordless glance from Father. Nothing more.

He *knew*. Or did he? Didn't he? He couldn't know. Could he? Zosia brought me home that morning. She told him that we had been watching a film in her apartment and we fell asleep. Father was angry, but he trusted me more with another girl. He remembered my tears from losing Neela and Mother. He kept himself distant from me. Tadhg was his only confidante after losing Mother. He must have felt I couldn't understand, had never lost a lover. But I did. I did understand. He had no idea how it felt to have the one person who gave you these weird animal parts and who was supposed to help you deal with it just abandon you because of something you did.

I took a slow sip of my coffee as I sat on my bed. Bitter like the aftertaste of sex. Is that what I had? Sex and *ganja*. Sex with a boy. Mother should be proud, right?

I missed him already. Despite Zosia's repeated declarations that Gio was an absolute ass, a player, but not sweet like Petru. He was mean, and I hadn't been around him long enough to see it. I shouldn't want him ever again. Although I knew she was probably right, my body wondered how he entered and left so soon when even the walls seemed to beat with his rhythm. His body extended harmoniously into the pliant mattress, down to the floor, across to the walls, upward, in, down, again. A circle. A circle is always easy to disappear into. If you let it move fast enough: whirlpool. Time can do that, too. Fast is hallucinogenic, effortless once everything is moving together. Me: with a ruptured body like my ruptured soul.

Winter in Venice. It was a soul-winter, too. Full of rain. It felt strange to wear jumpers again. Thick woolen material covering my arms, chest, back. Corduroys on my legs. Zosia and I spent most of our time together. She had efficiently removed Gio from my life by kicking him out of the apartment. Another woman who kept to herself moved in. Zosia took me out for fish to celebrate. She was tougher than I imagined when I saw her for the first time in that red velvet dress. She typically wore black army pants with a fitted T-shirt and her hair in two long braids swinging with the wind.

I didn't care about Gio but I missed his body. Any body close to mine. When the skin is that close, it's easy to pretend that it belongs, it should be there, it is an extension of my own skin. I settled for the friendly touches I received from Zosia, though it didn't quell my desire. She tried to set me up with boys and I couldn't tell her otherwise, couldn't say—I wanted breasts, beauty, softer skin, longer hair.

A boy took me to lunch once. I didn't mind the company, but I didn't feel like kissing him across from *La Giudecca* by the blue-covered gondolas on the water. I wrote: SORRY, I DON'T WANT TO KISS YOU.

He got angry. Asked me twice before writing CIAO and walking away. I laughed. Boys were so dramatic, like the mimes, the sea.

I walked out of my bedroom door one morning and bumped into Father.

What are you doing? Why are you standing here? I asked.

He opened his mouth and raised his hands as if to say something, then stopped.

What? I insisted.

Nothing. He finally responded and walked away.

I rushed out into the streets, curious but distracted by a meeting with Zosia. She had found a new source for getting *ganja* for us. She had always used Gio, but she didn't want to deal with him anymore. Getting high with her was different. I felt safe in her room or walking the streets beside her. *Ganja* was something Neela and I heard about in our village. We were told to avoid certain shops where men sold handmade clay pipes and smoked from them all day long. Those men always seemed so happy that I once asked Neela if she wanted to try it.

Never! She signed. *Smoking is very bad! Only men smoke here. Women are not allowed to smoke.*

I didn't understand why it was okay for only men but I listened to her because I didn't want to make her upset. Things were different here. *Ganja* wasn't so taboo and everyone seemed to do it. I knew that Mother wouldn't approve, but that's what made it so appealing. Neela couldn't see me here either.

It wasn't until after I turned sixteen that Zosia felt okay smoking with me. She wanted to preserve whatever innocence I had left after that night with Gio. I hadn't felt innocent for a long time, but I humoured her. Once we started smoking together, I felt so much more alive. I finally understood what all those Indian men were smiling about. Zosia liked to call Venice a wicked awesome place for getting high and wandering around.

W-i-c-k-e-d a-w-e-s-o-m-e. She fingerspelled.

I've told you that you don't need to spell out w-i-c-k-e-d a-w-e-s-o-m-e. It's the same sign as really great or really wonderful. They all mean the same thing!

No, girl. I need to fingerspell because the words are not the same. I want you to understand the exact word I mean! It's not just really great, it's w-i-c-k-e-d a-w-e-s-o-m-e.

You can show how great with face and size of sign, remember? I didn't want to say that the slowness of her fingerspelling annoyed me, especially when it was the same two words over and over. Zosia loved new English words and had overheard this phrase from an American tourist. Sometimes I wished I could overhear things. I wondered how often hearing people eavesdropped on other conversations. Wasn't that rude? They always assured me that it was something they couldn't control, but I wasn't convinced.

❧

Mid-February. Almost: *Carnivale*. Tourists flooded the islands even more than in summer. Everyone wore masks and danced through the streets celebrating Venice. It reminded me of the Hindu festivals Neela and I attended. There were always full moon festivals at the Shiva Temple to the south of our village. People went in masses. Incense filled the air with smoke—ghosts of gods rising up, circling the moon. Electric lights made the statues glow. Candles were placed inside tiny alcoves where the wind wouldn't snuff them out. Men played drums in the courtyards.

We held each other tightly as we walked past the drummers into the blackened corridors of the inner temple. Red and white powder on our foreheads. The black statues of the gods felt alive—ghosts who would rise and become smoke. I swear we heard their whispers, their spirits moving through the insides of our saris as they passed us with the wind. The crumbling walls seemed to have mouths, opening, daring us to fall into their cracks.

Carnivale had its own ghosts and gaps as well. For the entire two weeks, I walked around in a red cape wearing a burgundy, gold, and white cracked-marble style mask. Black lines around my eyes. Red *punjabi* underneath. Zosia wore a tight black velvet dress, green mask, gold swirls on her cheeks. I traced my fingers along her arm as we walked the streets—a masquerade of masks and bodies moving awkwardly around each other. With her, I felt safe. Every night was a glare of red, orange, blue, green, yellow, black. Cream and white doll faces. Some people had long wooden stilts beneath their cloaks that made them eight or nine feet tall. I liked to stare up at them. They were my red and black angels. Neela would have been one of them.

One night we drank a bottle of wine between us on a dock. I forgot this was my *friend*. This was *Zosia*, a girl who loved Petru, a girl who loved boys. Instead, I stared at her green painted skin, her red painted lips, and I just wanted—

She was laughing as she reached out and touched me along my arm. Her hand slid up to my neck, stroking it, until I couldn't contain myself anymore. I reached out, pulled her face to mine, and kissed her. The hard skin of our masks rubbed and hit against each other, but her lips were soft and rich. Her breath smelled like our merlot. I pulled her down onto me.

My mask's eyeholes only allowed me to see her. Her green and gold skin up close, her dark eyes staring at me. I never wanted to stop. I loved the dance of our tongues. Hands buried in each other's hair. Hers was so long it tangled me in its curls. I pulled it and she bit my lip. We laughed. She pulled away, lifted the bottle of wine to her lips, and led me down a narrow road along the water. As if nothing had happened. I wanted to grab her again, throw her against the walls of the apartments to our left, and kiss her green skin until my lips were green.

Back in her bedroom, we kept drinking and Zosia started touching me again. Friendly at first, but I wanted more. Everything she did was sexy to me. Her velvet dress was so soft against my skin that I almost didn't want to remove it. I thought of Neela, but this girl was different. I knew this wasn't true love. Zosia was laughing, she was green and gold, her wild hair spread over her sheets. I kissed her again. This time she pulled me back into her bed. My fingers pulled up her dress, reaching, exploring this new body, a new girl, searching for the skin within the fabric. I found it.

YEARNINGS

A grey dawn spread across the room. My head pounded. I turned to Zosia's sleeping form beside me. The green of her face had rubbed off onto her pillows, her sheets, my hands, my shoulders, probably my face, too. What had we done? The night came back like a bad dream. She stayed on her back, I had taken off all her clothes, now in piles under the covers at our feet, and I had touched her in ways I vowed never to touch another woman. Never anyone except Neela. With this act, I wasn't just betraying her, I was betraying Mother, too. At least with Neela, I hadn't really known Mother's feelings. With Neela, I was doing it for love. Zosia didn't even want me, didn't want girls. I carefully climbed out of her bed and gathered my cape, mask, and shoes from the floor. Zosia was still asleep when I crept outside.

The alleyways and streets were scattered with broken masks, trash, and early morning wanderers like me. It looked like a hurricane had passed through. Father had fallen asleep again with the television on. I crept into my room and gently closed the door, then rushed under the covers. Hiding beneath my elephants, I tried not to feel unfaithful. Neela slept with that boy in the canyons, so I didn't think twice about my night with Gio. But this time I had touched another girl the way I used to touch her.

The last night of *Carnivale* arrived. I hadn't seen Zosia since the morning after we had sex. I couldn't avoid her any longer. She came to my apartment with her costume in her bag and once we were alone in my room, she signed, *What happened that night when we drank wine together? Did I do something wrong?*

I did something wrong, and I can't even admit it. I can't even tell you, I thought, before signing, *I'm tired. Maybe I'm sick. Nothing else. Sorry.*

Tonight, let's go out? No drink, just smoke?

She pulled out her pipe and held it out to me. I wondered if she even remember what happened in her bed. I tried to decline but the *ganja* tempted me. I wanted to feel giddy and free. I lit the incense to hide the smell and we both took a few hits while putting on our costumes for the last time.

An hour or so after we entered the streets, my world began to shift. Everyone was staring at me. Laughing, moving in and out, up and down. I was surrounded by all those people. I was holding hands with Zosia, but I felt alone. Words passed along the wind, between the bodies. Everything passed me by. Crowding me. I tried to look down at my feet moving thousands of inches away along the stone streets. Everyone staring: disembodied eyes surrounded in shades of red, orange, cracked-marble, gold, silver, blue. I felt their eyes and they made me invisible. I was underwater and it had been over thirty minutes. Another second of this and I wouldn't be able to hold my breath any longer. Suffocated by the masked smiles. Painted gold. Silver. Swirling, turning—until Zosia was pulling me along, into her apartment, away from the crowds, the masks, the bodies everywhere.

She signed: *Are you ok? You looked nervous so I thought it would be better here.*

I signed, *Yes. I felt weird with everyone staring at me.*

As we got into her bed, I couldn't get the memories of that night out of my head. I had to tell her. I flipped the light back on and rubbed her arm to wake her. *Do you remember what happened in your bed that night?*

She smiled, nodded. *You were amazing! It was really fun. Have you ever done that before?*

The room shifted, tipped over into canyons, pools, elephant sheets. Fun was not the word I would use for it. No. It wasn't. *Yes.*

She read my face, her smiled died away and realisation dawned. *O-h, I'm so sorry! I didn't know! Why didn't you say anything before? Are you g-a-y? Or b-i?*

How to answer? When I didn't even know. *I think I'm gay. G-a-y. The sign is gay. But I don't know. I took advantage of you. I'm sorry.*

What? Took advantage? Fingerspell.

T-o-ok a-d-v-a-n-t-a-g-e.

No. You didn't do that! It was fine. I've never done that before, but I'm also not gay. I'm sorry.

It's ok. We are f-r-i-e-n-d-s. The sign is friends.

Friends. She repeated. *That's a good sign! Friends.*

She hugged me. Desire rose in my body, tingling from the vibration of skin against skin. I pulled away and signed: *I'm tired. I'm going to sleep now, ok?*

She nodded.

We turned the light off and lay down awkwardly side by side. I curled my body away from hers and ignored her warm breathing against the back of my neck. I fell asleep quickly, but instead of dreaming about Zosia or Neela, I dreamed about one autumn day when I was six and returning home from school. Father was distracted when he picked me up and didn't notice that I had been crying. As soon as we got home, I ran to Mother. She swept me up in her arms and I buried my face into her soft woolen jumper. It had different shades of blue like the sea. Her long hair draped over me like a curtain of warmth and safety. She held me until I pushed myself away far enough to sign, *The kids tease me. They're mean. I don't like school. I want to know more deaf kids like me. Hearing kids don't understand. Please?*

There were tears in her eyes when she replied, *I'm so sorry, baby. I will talk with your father. I don't want you to be unhappy. I love you.*

I dove back into the folds of her jumper and stayed there until my tears dried. She stroked my back and hair. She held me in a way that told me I could stay in her arms as long as I needed. She wouldn't let me go first.

I woke beside Zosia with a six-year-old child's yearning. I remembered that Mother always held me that way. She had never pulled away first, not until two months ago. I didn't understand how a mother could do that. How her love could suddenly be conditional. She wasn't successful with changing Father's mind about my school, but I dealt with it. On bad days, Mother held me, even after she returned to the sea. I ran to our beach or the rocks, and she would be there for me. On good days, I smiled at Father, even hugged him. Sometimes he took me for walks along the docks after school and we would look for the bottlenose dolphin of Dingle Harbor that the local fishermen had named "Fungie." Eventually I stopped hugging him, but I never let him hold me.

EARTH RISING

The day after the *Carnivale* ended, I walked into my apartment after having coffee with Zosia. I felt the vibration of Father's voice yelling as he signed: *What were you doing? Do you think this is a hotel? You can come home anytime and party every day because it's C-a-r-n-i-v-a-l-e? You've just turned 16, not 18!*

I didn't understand why he was suddenly angry when we had barely spoken since New Year's in Ireland. It was like, he'd forgotten he was my father for a while and now, today, he decided to remember.

You know I went out with Zosia. You acted fine with it before! What suddenly happened? You thought—o-h—maybe I'll yell at my daughter today! I'm not running away again. I don't care what you think!

He looked at me from across the room. His eyes were tired as if he had stayed up all night. He was wearing blue sweatpants and an old T-shirt. His coffee mug was on the counter next to a new pack of cigarettes. Our trip to Ireland had only made him smoke more. I suddenly remembered that he hadn't smoked while I was a child until she left us but I was too angry to ask him about it now. I stormed into my room and slammed the door behind me.

The next morning I walked into the kitchen and sat next to him at the table. He was reading a novel and drinking coffee. He looked up at me and there was only a slight trace of frustration in his eyes. No matter how much coffee he drank, he always looked tired. I waited to see if he had anything to say before asking, *Why didn't you smoke when mother lived with us? I remember now that you started smoking after she went back into the ocean.*

He looked down at the pack of cigarettes on the table and the small glass ashtray he carried around with it. *She hated smoking. It's not natural. I smoked once in front of her and she freaked out. I never did it again. Not until she left us. Do you want me to stop?*

I didn't expect him to ask that. *No.* I signed. *You can smoke, Dad, I don't care. I'm gay.*

What? What does the sign gay mean?

I hadn't realised he wouldn't have known that sign. Growing up, that wouldn't have been in my vocabulary with him, even though my school interpreters had shown me the sign when other kids were making fun of each other. *G-a-y.* I clarified.

He blinked, raised his eyebrows, and narrowed his eyes. He eventually said, *Is that why you were so angry when we left India? Were you with Neela?*

I hadn't wanted him to make that connection so immediately. Seeing her name in the air hurt me, as if she was here in this room, watching us, knowing what I had done. I nodded, stood up, and walked away even though I had planned to tell him exactly why Mother rejected me. In Ireland I had lied to him. I told him we had argued and I said the wrong things.

Father didn't sign to me much after that day but he didn't seem to be judging me either. He looked at me with compassion whenever I accidentally made eye contact with him. We took turns cooking or ordering food but we never ate meals together. I imagined he was happy when I didn't sign to him except to ask what kind of pasta he wanted.

When it became warmer, Father bought a canoe for fishing. He started taking me with him. Every time I went he caught too much. We had to stop after an hour. He didn't want to kill so many fish. I knew him as a fisherman, but the guilt in his eyes every time he caught even one fish was foreign to me.

One day, we were sitting in the canoe out in the bay. It was sunset and the air was chilly. The white churches of Venice glowed in the distance as I watched the gondolas and tourist boats glide through the calm waters. Father tapped me on the shoulder and signed: *It's ok that you're gay.*

I nodded and quickly turned away so that he wouldn't see my tears. I was angry that it had taken him this long to say this to me. I was pissed that it was *him* saying it, and not *her,* when Mother had accepted my deafness so much more than he did. How could she support that and not this? Why didn't he care that I wasn't happy with my school? I couldn't ask him these things, nor tell him about Mother. We sat in the boat with our hands down for a while before paddling back to the dock.

෴

One evening we ate gelato while sitting on the edge of a canal and looking at the water. Father signed: *I never gave you a birthday gift.* My birthday had been a month earlier, but we were both still feeling awkward after losing Mother. I had told him I didn't want to celebrate. I got high with Zosia. *What would you like as a gift?*

I wanted Mother to love me again. I wanted Neela. India. Another night in bed with Zosia. I wanted to hug Petru. Pet Casanova. Myself? My heart? Anything but that. Father meant something material, something he could give. I didn't have an answer, so I made one up. *The mountains? Maybe we can go see the A-l-p-s?*

I surprised myself with the idea, but I had never really seen mountains. Never been to the Himalayas. The only mountains I saw were the highest peaks of Ireland, but they weren't the Alps. They didn't have snow-covered peaks even in springtime. I had always wanted the sea. Maybe there was something in the mountains that I didn't know.

Ok. Once the school year is finished, we can take a train up to the mountains. Does that sound good?

I smiled and nodded.

A vacation with Father was a strange prospect. Before I could worry about what we would do or say to each other alone in the mountains, the smooth train ride put me to sleep. Father shook me awake when we could see the beginnings of the Alps around us. They looked like giant chunks of Earth rising as if from an unseen force, a heartbeat deep inside the dirt. It wouldn't let them sit, wouldn't let them rest, until they had reached the stars. I had never before wanted to rise high up above everything. Never wanted to fly.

The train rode along impossible bridges connecting the middles of two mountains. A few times we drove through a mountain and came out on the other side. These were foothills. In the distance along the horizon, there were massive white and black jagged rocks pushing against the blue that seemed to hold up the sky. Down below, along the valleys of bright green, a clustered town of tiny stone and dark wooden homes, with its one grey church tower rising up, a mini mountain itself with its crucified wooden peak. From such a distance, the villages here looked like places where tiny gnomes lived.

We stayed in a small town on the side of a mountain with a wide view of the valley. A river ran through it like a snake. Neela would be that long dark blue shining body cutting through the belly of the fields. Crystal clear, nourishing water. This remote place next to the stars reminded me of Heaven. People here smiled from the heart while offering you bread and cheese and the warmth of a fire in the dark. I think Father felt it, too. Sometimes the sea was too rough, but here, when the wind was violent, there was always a home built into the mountain itself, with fire and soup and blankets to keep warm. The sea didn't have that. Any boat could get tipped if a wave decided to be a mountain.

I wanted to stay up there forever. The people had patience only country people had. They lived on Mountain Time, so they never got upset with trying to communicate with me. Nobody got angry when I couldn't read their lips and they realised they had to write things down. Nor when they realised I couldn't speak. My Italian was rudimentary but good enough to read basic things. Some people knew English.

One day we hiked up to the top of the foothill mountain where our town was nestled, and saw the giant Alps rising behind it. They looked two-dimensional and unreal. We sat against a pine tree, drinking water and eating fruit. Father turned to me. *Are you happy here?* I nodded. *We are always near the sea. How do you feel being up so high?*

It's a little scary but so beautiful.

When my father died, my mother brought me to see the White Mountains. New H-a-m-p-s-h-i-r-e. Have you heard of that place?

I drew a map of America in the air. *Boston is here. N-H is here, right?*

Yes. My mother and I hiked there. I loved the mountains but I always loved the sea more. I'm not sure why. The sea is filled with another world. Mountain tops overlooking our world aren't mysterious enough for me maybe.

I was surprised to watch him sign this way. As if he were speaking with Tadhg. I looked down, ran my fingers through the velvety moss underneath me. Edged away from him, or maybe I was edging away from my own unchangeable preference for the sea. I wanted to love something else: these mountains, the bridges between, the gaps, the snow, the pines, the sap sticking to my fingers as I traced brown lines of it along the body of the tree. He reached out and held my hands. I almost pulled away, but I looked into his eyes. They were red-rimmed, watery. He lifted one hand to sign: *There's something I must tell you.*

The gentle wind picked up and stopped. I waited.

Long ago, back home, a man hurt you. Do you remember?

My breath faltered. I pulled my hand away, stood up suddenly. *How do you know? What do you mean?*

I felt too naked—standing that way, between the tree and the edge of the cliff, far-away snow frozen to the rocks. I sat back down, pulled my legs in, knees to my chest, eyes darting, watching him. There was nowhere else I could go. I prayed to Kali. Felt her rising up behind me, her red tongue hanging, skulls smiling, scythe clasped in her palm. My breath slowed back down as he continued.

You had nightmares. Do you remember? You woke me every time. I watched. Forgot to breathe. *You screamed in sign in your sleep, do you understand? I couldn't handle it. I was angry. I wanted to fix you. Help you. I found out who did it.* He paused. Searched my eyes. I didn't blink. Waited. *I beat him and threw his body into the sea. He's dead now. Tadhg helped me to make sure it looked like an accident. That's why I've been so secretive. That's why I hid from you whenever I spoke with Tadhg. It's the real reason why we left Ireland. I couldn't stay there.*

I felt Kali smiling, but I couldn't. I remembered the last few months in Ireland, Father's sudden closeness and his sudden distance. I didn't care. I just wanted Mother. Wanted to stay home, even though I realised that moving away, moving to India, was a way for me to move on, too. Escape. Kali ran the scythe along my backbone. Reminding me of the strength she gave, her red power that extended all along the dirt. She could reach through the Earth itself, rise out of the Alps behind me—something my real mother, however much I wished for her, could never ever do.

Now Father waited, his own larger knees pulled up to his chest, a curling red lock of stray hair hanging in his face. I tried to think about right and wrong, but between Father sitting before me, the wide trunk of the silent tree beside me, and the bloody force of Kali behind me—I couldn't think what he did was wrong at all.

Thank you.

I had questions, but now was not the time. I was glad he didn't volunteer more information. He had told me more than enough for now. As we walked back down the steepest part of the trail, I was looking ahead across the valley at its thousand shades of green. Father was behind me. Kali had left to wander the snow peaks, screaming battle calls across the rocks, drawing out the gods that lived there. Suddenly I slipped on the wet moss, my back slammed to the ground as gravity pulled me downward. Rocks banged against my body. My hands reached for branches, anything to hold onto, but they kept grasping handfuls of grass and dirt. A stick stabbed me through the webbing in my left hand as I kept falling. Everything was hard, dirty, wet. Scraping. Nothing like the thick water of the sea.

The trail turned sharply to the right, open space ahead—air, a cliff plunging down—I thrust my hands out. They finally caught the base of a small mountain pine. I held it so tightly that I felt my hands growing numb. I was lightheaded, gasping, my face flat against the dirt and rock. I watched ants crawling. The ants prompted me to lift my head and see exactly how close I came to the edge.

My sneakers dangled in the air. I didn't have the energy to lift myself up or pull my feet back onto the ground. I felt Father rushing towards me from above and prayed he wasn't going to fall, too. I felt his arms, reaching around my chest, lifting me, dragging me upward. He sat down on the trail with my body lying across his lap.

My face pointed back down again, I looked up, turned over, pain shooting from—ribs, elbows, knees, hands. My left hand was bleeding from where the stick pierced the web between my ring finger and my pinkie. Nothing had ever done that before. Father grabbed my hand and examined it like the doctor he wasn't. He reached into his back pocket, pulled out a handkerchief, and wrapped my hand in it. We watched the spreading red stain through the whiteness of the fabric. I looked up into his eyes.

He was terrified. As soon as our gazes met, he pulled me to his chest, squeezing my battered body. I didn't care that it hurt. I started crying without wanting to, without understanding why. I was fine. I was fine. I was fine.

We spent the rest of our time in the Alps by the fireplace in our guesthouse. The round woman who owned it fawned over me. I felt like a patient in a strange mountain hospital. The owner and Father brought me thick soups with bread and warm cheeses. Hot teas, hot coffee. They spread the window curtains so that I could see the giant mountains beyond, that wonderful rising Earth that almost tipped me inside it forever.

I had never felt wanted by the Earth, but as I fell down that trail, I felt the Earth itself pulling me urgently, as if she wouldn't have given up until I was swallowed, smothered, buried in rocks, moss, roots. I wanted roots, right? Maybe the Earth was trying to give them to me. Plant me here—in these mountains. Far from the turmoil of the sea, the wild Indian gods with blue and red skin, far from the lovers I couldn't have, the mother I couldn't please, and the avenging father I had always hated. Saved by a small pine tree shorter than myself, rescued by a guilty father who made me cry, made me feel weaker than I was, who carried me down the rest of the trail even though I probably could have walked. Nothing was broken, just twisted, bruised, cut. *Nothing serious*, I pleaded, trying to make them all go away—

these helpers. I wanted to wander the village again, but they wouldn't have it. They kept me by the fire like an armchair growing old and dusty. Healing, scabbing over, a left hand whose web I couldn't spread.

HANDS TELLING STORIES

The train back to Venice was long. I couldn't sleep. I felt so calm that I didn't need to close my eyes. When we returned to our familiar streets and canals, golden crosses and churches, everything glowed a bit less. Even the mint rice coloured walls of our apartment appeared faded. The black railings of our balcony—dull.

I missed the majesty of snow. The rivers of sap down the thick pine trunks. Grass spreading out across whole valleys, not just contained in a park like an animal in a zoo. Wilderness. Forests. Waterfalls tumbling below precarious bridges. My body tumbling down the trail. I was pulled by the Earth, desired. My wounds had mostly healed. I had a few scabs I tried hard not to peel off and uncover the tender pink beneath. I wanted to climb back up past all that green and brown, towards the wide-open blue and white of the sky.

Instead, I was back on the islands covered in manmade sculptures, manmade homes, paved roads hiding the Earth from my eyes, my skin. I think Father felt out of place, too. We both stuck around the apartment for a few days, ordered takeout, and drank coffee side by side on the balcony. It took me three days to ask him.

How did you find out who r-a-p-e-d me?

He was sitting alone on the balcony smoking a fag. He coughed and put it out on the bottom of his chair. I sat beside him and waited.

Your mother helped me.

What?! Those were the last words I ever expected him to say. *I thought you never saw her! Are you saying you did go and see her after she left? After she became a seal again?*

Of course, I did. She was my wife. I know who she was. She watched over you for me when you went out on the rocks. She had seen that man walking along the rocks, too. She saw him with other girls. She never saw him rape anyone. Tadhg and I saw him in the pubs a lot. He wasn't from here and he didn't look right to us.

Does Tadhg know what he did to me?

Yes. He had to know. Why would he help if he didn't know? He was just as angry as I was. He felt for you. I remembered Tadhg watching me sometimes. He always had kindness in his eyes, and since he told me about his wife, I did feel close to him. *He's the only one who knows.*

What about Mum? I never told her. Why didn't she tell me that she knew?

We thought it was better not to tell you. We knew you weren't ready to talk about it because you didn't come to us. Your mother helped me kill him.

How did she help?

Tadhg brought the man and me out on the ferry one night. We drank together and pretended to be friends. We beat him to death and your mother dragged the body far down into the sea. No one missed him. He was a stranger to us. He bothered other young girls. Many of the people in our town didn't like him. But I still felt guilty. I was scared someone would find out I killed him. I wanted to take you far away from there and Tadhg agreed with me. He wasn't afraid. He didn't have anything else to lose by staying. Your mother didn't want me to take you away from her but eventually she said ok because she didn't want you orphaned if I was ever found out. We didn't want you in a foster home. Do you understand?

Why are you telling me this now? Why didn't you tell me before? I wished he had said something. This changed everything, changed him in my eyes. I wasn't sure who this man was anymore, even if some part of me now loved him more, loved him differently.

He stared at the water for a while before responding.

I wasn't sure how to tell you. I wanted to tell you but things were hard. I needed to be away from you for a while, but I didn't want to be away from you. He took my hand in his own. His calloused palms scratched against my skin. *I didn't want to leave you in India. But I also didn't know how to be around you without telling you what I did. I thought you were too young to know about it. You weren't even a teenager yet. Don't you understand?* He signed with one hand, eyes filled with pleading.

How did you deal with it? How did you feel after killing someone?

He dropped my hand and ran his fingers through his hair. His hands were trembling slightly when he replied. *It felt strange. H-a-u-n-t-i-n-g. I still have dreams about it. I see Tadhg, the man's body, your mother. But he hurt you and he hurt other girls. I can't feel as if his death was wrong. I just wish the blood wasn't on my hands. When you have a child*—I raised my eyebrows—*I mean if you have a child*—he smiled—*you will understand what I'm saying. You'll do anything to protect your children.*

I could imagine that. If anything like that had happened to Neela—if she had been raped—I probably would have killed them, too. I remembered the fish. *Is that why you get upset when you kill fish? Does it remind you?*

He nodded.

Then why do we go fishing? It didn't make sense to me that he would continue to do something if it upset him.

Because I'm responsible for what I did. It reminds me, but that's a good thing. I need to remember. And fishing is peaceful. It's ok if it's painful, too. Do you understand?

I saw Zosia in my head. I began to wonder if I kept smoking *ganja* with her because I felt less pain over losing Neela. The *ganja* made things easier. Every thought I had felt lighter. I didn't worry about Neela. I just enjoyed my time with Zosia, even if it didn't involve sex. Smoking made me feel warm and happy. I wanted to give this feeling to Father. He deserved it more than I did, didn't he? Sometimes the guilt I had felt for loving Neela enough to lose Mother was worse than the feeling of having been raped. The stranger wasn't supposed to love me. What he did hurt me but guilt was something worse because it had to do with something I did—a way that I hurt someone else. *Dad, have you ever smoked ganja?*

He laughed at me. The smile looked so weird on his face that I laughed, too. His eyes narrowed. *Why do you say that? Do you smoke ganja now?*

I didn't know what to say but I was sure the way I fidgeted around in my chair was enough of an admission. I thought that he would yell at me again.

Does it help you? Does smoking ganja make you feel better?

I thought for a while before signing: *I thought so. But now that you're asking me that question, I think not really. The pain is still there. I can't just smoke ganja all day, every day and be numb to it.*

Good. He smiled. *Maybe now I don't have to steal your pipe or follow you around to make sure you're not smoking ganja, like a good father, huh?*

I smiled back uncomfortably. I knew he was joking outright, but deep down I was scared he actually might do what he was suggesting. The risks he had taken for me, the crimes he committed, the distance and the secrets he kept made him feel reckless to me. Powerful. He was capable of anything and I began to admire him for it. Still—*Can I have a fag?*—I tested.

No fucking way. If you want these, I'll just throw them out. Ok?

Ok. I stood up slowly, grabbed his hands, and pulled him up next to me. I hugged him. I wasn't sure what else to do, and I needed to feel his body confirm the affection his words demonstrated. This was another test. I kept hugging him and waiting for him to let go, waiting for him to push me away first.

After what felt like many minutes, he stroked my back but still held me. I felt love inside his arms in a way that I never had with him before. Not even in Ireland after I saved him. The love hurt because it reminded me of all the times I stayed away from him. Time we lost. A million other thoughts ran through my mind. I had to step back. I had to let go and take a walk.

I'll be back later, ok? Thank you for talking with me.

You're welcome. Anytime. Please come talk to me again soon?

Ok. I turned and left him standing in the sunlight.

An hour later I was walking past the train station when I felt a rush of fur against my legs. Thick nails clawed at me. I looked down and tried to lift Casanova's large body off the ground. My wet lips smiled as he licked them. I looked up and there he was: tall, lanky Petru. Wearing jeans and a black T-shirt that fit his body perfectly. Shining midnight eyes. Hair pulled back with a few stray curls. I leaped into his arms. Casanova clawed at our legs as he held me, but neither of us cared. He put me back on my feet and suddenly it dawned on me. Had he gone home first? Had he seen her yet? I was torn between them, caring so much for them both. Regretting that night with Zosia and feeling ashamed for liking Petru, too.

Petru's mime-wisdom caught my guilty face. But he didn't have anything to write with, so he tried to act out a father reprimanding his daughter, which did nothing but made me feel the flush rising in my cheeks. He could do nothing else but usher me back to his apartment. I hoped Zosia was out. I didn't know how to be in the presence of both of them. My stomach tightened as we walked and I played with Casanova to distract myself.

When we stepped into an empty apartment, I let out such a large sigh that Petru gave me a look with one eyebrow arched as he searched for a pen and paper. OK CRAZY GIRL, WHAT DID I MISS?! WHAT'S WRONG?

I pointed to his room, and I sat down to write when we were safe behind his closed door with Casanova beside us.

There's so much to tell you. I signed without thinking, but so far he understood. I looked into his eyes, and I wanted to tell him everything. I wanted him to sort everything out for me, save me like he did when I first came to this city. But I knew he couldn't.

Z-o-s-i-a told me about you and her. About you and other women. Then I was attracted to her. She was beautiful. We got drunk and had sex. I'm sorry.

I wasn't sure why I was telling him this. He didn't understand most of my signing, so I had to write it down. I didn't want to cause him pain, but a part of me was angry with him for what he'd done to Zosia. I wanted him to feel the same thing she felt. The look in his eyes showed me I succeeded. I also saw that what he was feeling for me was something else I knew: a memory framed in red canyons. Containing naked bodies, dark skin. I wanted to drown. My world, once again, tipped over into the sea.

Only love could do such things. But this time it wasn't my broken heart. I looked down at my body: green T-shirt, loose black pants, necklace of sacred beads laying across my small breasts, my messy locks of dark auburn hair, tiny silver Ganesh charm hiding between cotton and skin. Webbed hands. Webbed feet that couldn't wear flip-flops without pain. What was compelling about this body? How could he possibly want me more than her? Or be angry at me for having her when he kept throwing her away?

I left the apartment and walked down the street. Bright sunset stained the sky red and pink. The world was still fuzzy. I could barely make out the outlines of the buildings, their black railings, uneven stone walls, and flowered window sills. The horizon lines around me shifted into palm trees as if I were back inside my Bay of Bengal, swimming frantically to the shore with the same red sun setting behind the line of trees. How my worlds had overlapped: India with Venice. Where was I? Or was I all of them, together, entwined? How to live on land and in sea? With love and without?

A week later, in the park on the eastern edge of Venice, I saw them. Petru and Zosia walked hand in hand through the grass with Casanova trailing behind, sniffing every blade, every fallen leaf. Petru was laughing, nudging her. She jumped sideways and jumped back. Her hair was flying behind her as she leapt into his arms, smothering him with her lips, her face against his neck. It was clear that they should be together. I felt it in their gestures. His hand across her cheek was delicate. Was he really this way with every woman? I was green with envy. I wanted what they had. I wanted to be him. I wanted to be her.

Sitting in the damp grass, I leaned my face in to smell it. Dirt and rain. Stray bits of fallen petals and leaves. I lay down against the ground with my arms stretching out, holding the Earth between them. I wanted Neela to rise up out of the Earth like Kali. As I lifted my body up, I only saw a red face, hanging tongue, smiling skulls dangling, scythe lying in the grass. I looked back towards the lovers, but they were gone.

⁂

I was drinking coffee and reading Shakespeare's *Hamlet* in a café near Father's apartment. Daydreaming of Ophelia in a willow tree. Zosia rushed up and embraced me. She sat down across from me and signed, *Where have you been? I've missed you! P-e-t-r-u is here again. He told me about the girls he fucked and I cried, but he said he was sorry. He wants to date me again but I need to go slow. Do you think I'm stupid for even considering it?*

I don't know. I can't judge you. I felt awkward and out of place as her confessor. I wasn't sure how to be close to her and Petru at the same time. There were so many feelings I had inside.

I don't understand why he fucks other girls. I admitted.

I don't know either. He's a lover boy. She smiles sadly.

I wanted a lover again. Any lover. Girl. Boy. Any skin against mine. Instead, I signed, *Do you want me to talk to him?*

Yes! Will you? Thank you! I think he must still cheat on me. How could he stop himself, but I don't know for sure. You'll find out for me?

Yes, I'll try. I understand how you feel. It had taken me so long to trust Neela again, and for months, I still saw the bodies, the red canyon walls, the back with the hand moving, the hand that said *sorry* as if it could change what was happening inside my own body, or between their bodies, erase the betrayal.

I found Petru easily enough. After seeing him with Zosia, I didn't understand why he hadn't tried to see me again. He acted like I broke his heart, and then he fawned over her as if he loved her truly, completely. If he was lying—

Hi. I waved.

He walked over to me in the courtyard when I met him. Is he lying now? Would he look at me as he did?

How are you? I ventured.

Ok. His eyes were blank and his face more serious than I had ever seen.

What's really going on with you? What happened to our friendship?

You fucked my girlfriend.

I told you we were drunk! She wasn't your girlfriend; she just wanted to be your girlfriend! She told me that! You've never been faithful to her so what gives you the right to be angry with us for this?

He was confused. I had to write: YOU LEFT HER. YOU WEREN'T HER BOYFRIEND WHEN I WAS WITH HER. SHE'S BEEN SO UPSET BECAUSE YOU'VE NEVER BEEN FAITHFUL TO HER. WHY? AND HOW CAN YOU POSSIBLY BE

UPSET AT US WHEN YOU CHEAT ON HER ALL THE TIME?

He looked angry. He stared into my eyes and we sat down on the steps of the familiar church. Petru reached for the pen: I'M SORRY. YOU ARE RIGHT. I DO NOT OWN HER. I AM JEALOUS. I FALL FOR YOU. I FALL EASY. I LOVE ZOSIA, IN SOME WAY, BUT IT HARD TO STAY WITH HER. I WANT STAY BUT SHE MAKE ME FEEL IN TRAP. YOU YOUNG, MORE EASY. WE FOCUS ON COMMUNICATION. I HELP YOU. ZOSIA TOO SMART. I NOT HELP HER.

I'm stupid?! My hands burst out. *This is all bullshit, you're just scared! Wait. What?!*

I wrote furiously: I AM NOT STUPID. YOU ARE STUPID. THIS IS BLOODY BULLSHIT. YOU'RE JUST SCARED. AND YOU'RE BEING SELFISH! YOU NEED TO PICK ONE PERSON, ZOSIA, OR JUST STOP EVERYTHING AND GO AWAY. DATE A MILLION OTHER GIRLS, BUT LEAVE US ALONE!

I got up and walked away, but he grabbed me. Pleaded. Wrote again: YOU NOT STUPID! JUST MORE EASY. I DON'T KNOW. I AM STUPID. I DON'T WANT TO LOSE ZOSIA. I WANT HER. WHAT DO I DO? HOW DO I NOT LEAVE? HOW I STAY, NO TRAP?

I breathed deep. Stared at the Petru I thought was perfect. Now he just looked lost and afraid. But I would never be afraid. I didn't understand fear anymore. Kali smiled behind me, lying on the stones, laughing. I ignored my own jealousy—that he had chosen her over me. But I could make things better by helping them, right? I had chosen Neela long ago. I shouldn't want him or Zosia. I grabbed some cloth and began to tie it over his eyes. He panicked, signing and voicing: *Wait wait stop, what are you doing?*

Trust me. We're going to walk now while you are blindfolded.

He looked at me, searching my eyes. Yet when I started to blindfold him again, he let me do it. I stood up, held his hands, and pulled him up next to me. Casanova darted ahead of us through the crowds. I kept his hands in mine, walked backwards for a minute to watch him. His body resisted. I felt it in the pressure of his fingers. I know he heard people around us. I turned around and pulled him with one hand behind my back. People moved out of our way when they saw his blindfold. A few people pushed past us. Petru tripped and almost fell down, but I caught him. We walked for an hour or so. Through crowds, over bridges, my hand holding his, skin against skin. I felt the speed of his heart beating fast, but eventually it slowed down.

I didn't stop until I felt him walking behind me in tune with my every motion. Comfortable in his blindness. I led him to the side of the canal, a far off courtyard from where we started. I sat for a while, watching him. Casanova came and licked our faces. Petru and I smiled at each other. I untied him and he hugged me. We sat in silence, our hands in our laps.

Have you been cheating? I asked him as we stood up.

What does the sign cheating mean?

CHEATING, I wrote. His eyes turned away from the paper quickly. I slapped him, forced him to look me in the eye and glared. *Will you stop please? Or break it off with Z-o-s-i-a?*

He stood silently for a while before writing: I WILL STOP WITH OTHER GIRLS. THEY DON'T MATTER TO ME. I AM STILL SCARED OF SERIOUS RELATIONSHIP BUT WILL TRY, OK?

Ok. I smiled and hugged him goodbye. I decided not to tell Zosia. They deserved a real chance, and if I told her I knew she might never be able to stay with him. I didn't want more lovers to separate in anger or pain. I had seen enough of that already.

For the rest of the summer, I never saw Petru without Zosia by his side. They seemed truly content with each other. Sometimes seeing them made me think about my parents, and I had to go off by myself for a while. It was hard to imagine such things anymore: a mother on land, a mother human, and a father not alone, a father happy. Other times I saw Neela in her best sari, standing in a crowd of tourists, beckoning to me. Neela next to the basilica, surrounded with the grey and violet wings of pigeons, her dark hair blowing in the wind like crows.

There were moments with Petru and Zosia when words rose to my wrists: *love, ants, red canyons, selchie, Neela*. Regardless of my hands yearning to spell out their anguish, I couldn't. The memories sunk back down along my bloodstream. Back into my box-shaped heart—went inside single file like school children. Locked. Key: swallowed and left to rest in my belly, thick with tar-like memory-blood.

In the evenings Father and I shared secrets. I told him about Neela. *She's waiting for me. She's waiting.*

He looked at me with the eyes of someone whose lover had not waited. I knew he hoped for me, even if it meant losing me. He knew how much power love had over our ability to be happy. He didn't want me to end up like him. Across the table, his hand reached for mine. I took it awkwardly.

When did you get that tattoo? I pointed to the wave on the back of his calf.

He let go of my hand. *It was years ago in B-a-l-i. You know what the ocean means to me. That wave was something I drew while on the ship.*

It's cool. I signed, thinking of designs in my head. Other ways I could be unnatural. A nose ring, like Neela. Maybe even a tongue ring. I thought of asking Father if I could do something like that soon—before turning 18—but I didn't. I decided to wait. A year and a half, that's all it would take. I had already saved half of my plane fare to India. The money was stored in a special box in my wardrobe behind my jumpers from Ireland. It was wrapped in the sari top I wore to Venice, held tight against the heart I removed in order to keep it safe.

That black top with lace trim was my first sari top. Neela and I had gone to the tailor's house together. The tailor told us to raise our arms and stand still as she measured our busts and we tried not to giggle. Her toddler ran around the shop with bits of fabric in his hands, pulling at our *punjabi* pants whenever he got close. The walls of her shop and home were deep brown, as if they had been made with mud from another country—not this one, which had red dirt. Brown was the colour of Neela's body. Her hair, her eyes, her skin. They were all shades of brown and I had never loved the colour brown before, never wanted to fold myself inside it without caring whether I saw other colours ever again. Brown became every colour.

That autumn, Petru told me of his decision to stay in Venice for the winter, even if he couldn't find work, and I decided to tell him about Mother. He had already examined the extra skin between my fingers. We were comfortable enough for that. I could give him my hands. He gave me his. Just hands against hands against hands. Our language. Our safe touches. A way to send our thoughts back and forth like currents. Electric fingertips.

But I had different hands. He played with them. Spread them out like a frog. Amphibian. No. More like a seal, slight webs, nothing to worry about. No reason to be alarmed. My body. The sea. The place where I could catch it: that sea. How I could climb through it faster, merge with it, become one. How to explain? What words to describe hands—their tales? *These webs are here for a reason. My mother wasn't human. She was a s-e-l-c-h-i-e. Part s-e-a-l. She lives far away in the ocean. I have little parts of her. My webs. My nose can close and I can breathe for twenty minutes underwater without air. Do you think I'm crazy?*

Petru stood in front of me in a blue T-shirt, long hair pulled back, his large dark eyes staring. Did my hands tell their story right? They rested against my skirt, warm fabric against legs. Dark blue, pleated, waiting. Petru took my hands first, the hands he could touch. His dark skin against their pink whiteness. He held my two hands in his one. Signed with the other:

I don't know what to say. Back on Corsica, we have old stories, too, stories of sea people. I've never met one. His face smiled as his hand continued: *But I believe you.*

We smiled, embraced. My story—finished, told, accepted. The rest? Not yet. Not ready. Back into the time loop. Revolving. The pages of books. Journals. Poems. Sketches. Hands. Fabrics. Colours like yellow and orange and sometimes dark blue. Passing in a blur. Light. Dark. Sun up and down and up again. Stone figures with stone hands that tell no stories. Hands frozen in grey. Resting against their bodies that line the edges of buildings. White washed cement walls.

YELLOWED PAGES

When I turned seventeen, I slept with a couple boys from school. We spent our afternoons sneaking off to smoke *ganja* behind churches. I taught them dirty signs and we made out by the docks. I had understood something about Neela and Petru. The sex Neela had with boys wasn't love, and neither were the flings Petru had with other girls. Sometimes you had to have sex to know what sex was. If you knew what sex was, you knew what love was not. Maybe you were closer to knowing what love might be.

I never found love again after Neela. Not in those years in Venice. The boys were dirty and smelled of sweat and fish, or Italian seasoning. I swear I could smell basil and Parmesan when I kissed one of my boyfriends that year. His family owned a pizza place, and we ate there on Fridays after having sex in his vacant apartment while his parents were at the restaurant. I ate pizza every day for weeks until I couldn't stand it anymore and broke up with him. He wasn't even a friend, though. In Venice, I learned how to be a lover without actually loving someone. It freed me. Every time I had sex, it was like one more memory to erase the rape, or at least cause it to slowly fade away.

I was high the night I discovered what Father had really been writing. I had arrived home late, expecting him to be sleeping on the couch again. This time he was in his bed. I was excited to be able to lounge on the sofa and watch television by myself. I needed to wind down after having spent the evening working with Petru and Zosia in a mime show and having a post-work smoke as we wandered around. My legs were sore from all that movement but the *ganja* numbed my body from the pain. It was better than any painkillers I had ever taken. I was searching through the coffee table drawers for the jelly sweets Father liked to stash but I couldn't find them. I knew he had some in his bedroom somewhere. Sometimes deaf people are accused of being loud because we can't hear ourselves but the times I slipped out of the house with Neela had taught me to be quiet. If I moved slowly enough, I felt as if I could listen to my surroundings with my skin. The *ganja* only enhanced that sensation.

I was rummaging in a corner of his room and found the sweets stuffed between two piles of books. I noticed one titled *How to Craft Your Fiction Novel* and another titled *Character Construction and Plot*. He had told me he was writing about the coral reefs he studied in Indonesia. *Boring,* he signed. The fact that he didn't want me to read it until it was finished made sense to me, so I never pushed him. I was so curious about what these books suggested he was actually writing that I almost forgot to be careful about noise. I searched the stack of books for papers with handwriting and found some pages bound together. I grabbed them and went back to the living room.

I forgot the television, the sweets, and my fizzy drink sitting on the coffee table as I carefully removed the rubber band and began to read. His handwriting was printed neatly across the line-less sheets of thin yellowed paper, and his sentences slanted downwards across the page. As I read them, I felt as if I was falling down, too.

AUGUST 23RD—

FIVE SHELLS FOR FIVE DAYS SINCE I LEFT NUALA.

I LEAN OVER THE EDGE OF OUR BOAT—MONITORING FISH—CAN'T GET HER EYES OUT OF MY HEAD.

AUGUST 30TH—

TWELVE DAYS. I'VE THROWN SHELLS OVERBOARD—DON'T WANT TO FEEL SO MANY SHARP THINGS AGAINST MY SKIN.

NUALA PICKED UP SHELLS ON THE BEACH ALL THE TIME. THEY SCATTERED ALL OVER OUR MOBILE HOME. IN MY MIND I SEE BRANNAGH PAINTING IT BLUE—HER SPECIAL WOODEN DOOR WITH A CIRCULAR WINDOW LIKE A ROUND MOON.

MEMORIES KNOCK AGAINST THE BOAT WITH THE WAVES. HER HAUNTING SCREAMS—SLEEPLESS NIGHTS—FINDING BRANNAGH— WATCHING HER DANCE—KNOWING NUALA WOULD BE THERE. I KNEW OF HER MEETINGS WITH HER MOTHER, BUT I COULDN'T ADMIT IT. I DIDN'T WANT OUR FAMILY TO BE TORN LIKE MY OWN FAMILY GROWING UP. THE LAST THING I EVER WANTED WAS TO BECOME A FISHERMAN LIKE MY FATHER. OR A FATHER WHO ALLOWED HIS DAUGHTER TO BE HURT.

WORKING WITH BRANNAGH WAS PAINFUL—AGREEING WITH HER—SEEING HER IN THE OCEAN—LIKE OUR FIRST MEETING. I WANTED TO DIVE IN WITH HER—STAY WITH HER—BUT SOMEONE HAD TO STAY WITH NUALA, EVEN IF OUR CRIME COULDN'T STOP HER NIGHTMARES—THE OILY BLOOD OF FISH REMINDS ME. ANY DEATH REMINDS ME.

HOW CAN I TELL HER WHAT WE DID? WITH BALA'S FAMILY, THERE IS NEELA—A SISTER. ANYONE IS BETTER THAN ME.

SEPTEMBER 3RD—

I CUT MY FINGER ON A STRAY PIECE OF SHELL AND BROUGHT IT TO MY LIPS—BLOOD IN MY MOUTH WAS COPPERY—BITTER—TELLING ME—MONSTERS CAN'T BE KILLED. EVEN DEATH DOESN'T STOP NIGHTMARES.

NOVEMBER 28TH—

I WANTED TO TELL HER WHY I LOVE INDIA BUT I DON'T REALLY KNOW—PROBABLY THE COLORS. IT'S AS COLORFUL AS A CORAL REEF BENEATH THE WAVES. BALA—WILD AND CAREFREE—HE WOULD HAVE MADE HER LAUGH.

DECEMBER 4TH—

FOURTEEN YEARS AGO I MET BRANNAGH. HER STUPID FUCKING MYTH. WHY SEVEN YEARS? WHY NOT FOURTEEN? WHY NOT TWENTY? ALL I DO NOW IS SMOKE AND FAIL NUALA. BRANNAGH PROBABLY HATES ME BECAUSE I DIDN'T TELL HER.

JANUARY 10TH—

NIGHT—AGAINST THE RAILINGS—STARING INTO DARK WATERS. EVERY SPLASH IN THE LIQUID DISTANCE IS MY WIFE—RETURNING—HERE TO TELL ME SHE NEVER LOVED ME AT ALL. I WAS A CURSE. SHE STAYED FOR A MYTH, NOT A MAN OR A DAUGHTER—I'M ONLY HERE BECAUSE

The rest of the page was torn off. I didn't want to read anymore because I had also felt those dark waters around me, those phantom splashes. I felt them more and more. The memory of Mother—closing in. I collected the yellowed pages back together, wrapped them in their rubber band, and placed them back under the fiction writing books in his room.

I had wanted to find what he was writing, not those journal entries. I cursed under my breath at the memories it brought up for me of India. A part of me wanted to go into my room and pull out all the letters Neela had written me over the past couple years. I loved to trace my fingers over her curved Tamil script. She wrote of school mostly and used some code phrases we had come up with before I left to tell me she loved me. She was paranoid of *Ammā* or someone else reading them. I told her to post them herself but she asked, *What if your father reads them?!* At that point, I didn't even care if he hated me for loving her, but I didn't say that. Instead I gave up and told her to write of the red canyons when she wanted to write about me. I wondered what was really going on over there, though. I knew she wouldn't write about anything important or real because of her paranoia. How could we communicate? I didn't tell her anything about sex or drugs or even Mother. What could I say about those things? That I had made decisions she wouldn't agree with? Getting her back for cheating on me? We were too far apart to even begin that conversation. Although I wasn't afraid of *Ammā* reading her letters, I was sure she might read mine if she saw them first, and if I used English, she would badger Neela for details. I wanted to touch her again.

That night I was the one who fell asleep on the couch. The next morning, I bought a different set of sheets. The memories the elephant sheets triggered were starting to hurt too much.

When I admitted to Father that I had seen the books on fiction writing he looked as if he expected my questions. *I was waiting for you to find me out,* he signed.

Why didn't you just tell me?

I wanted to keep it a secret as long as possible. I'm sorry. Writing is new for me. It's not a job. I don't have a publisher. I'm just writing for me. I saved money from my work in I-n-d-o-n-e-s-i-a. I have to find work again soon, though.

Where will you work? And when? What's your book about?

He smiled at my queries with a hint of worry in his eyes. *I'll find something. Maybe m-i-m-e work like you?* He laughed when my eyes widened with shock. *I'm joking. Don't worry. I have options. I just like the break I'm getting right now. I like writing.*

What about your book?

My book is about a fisherman falling for a mermaid. It's cheesy, I know, but . . .

For what felt like a long time, I couldn't respond. I saw Father not just as Father. He was a man. I spread out my fingers before him. *Why did you make me think you didn't believe my hands were from Mum because she was a seal woman?*

Just because I believe in the m-y-t-h doesn't mean I want to believe in it.

I was afraid that if your mother and I both showed you that the m-y-t-h was real, that you would think everyone believes it. But most people don't believe. Do you understand? I was trying to make you strong.

You really didn't think I could figure out the truth for myself?

Now I see that. Now I understand. When you were younger, I didn't understand a child's mind. I didn't know how much you could figure out for yourself. Do you forgive me?

I nodded. *Is that why you sent me to a Hearing school?* I couldn't hold back my tears. I could see this pained him, and of this I was glad.

You have to live in a Hearing world. I didn't think you would be ok if you went to a Deaf school.

But most people around me are Hearing! I can't escape the Hearing world! A Deaf school would be a place for me to relax and feel happy. I can't spend my life in school, but don't you want me to be happy for at least a while?

His eyes became red. *Are you never happy and do you hate life because you live in a Hearing world?*

No, that's not what I'm saying. I deal with it because I have to. When I find friends who want to sign, I'm happier. I'm ok. I wiped my eyes and walked out of the room, but he grabbed my arm and pulled me to him. He held me even though I struggled. After a few moments he let me go.

HALLOWEEN

Every Halloween when I was a child, Mother sang to me by the sea. She was always sad. Once before she left us, I got her to tell me why. She had looked at me with her way of looking through me and signed slowly. *Tonight has a very old meaning. It's the time when living creatures and dead creatures are close. If you're quiet enough, you can feel the dead creatures and even talk with them. That's what I do here. I sing and I listen to them.*

I cried. Her words scared me. *If you die, will you come see me on this night?*

Of course. I'll always come to see you.

I held her until my arms hurt. She stayed in my arms until they went slack. When I remember how tightly and how long I gripped her waist, I realise I must have bruised her but she never complained. In India, I had been afraid too. Afraid that if I ever felt her or saw her somehow, it would mean she was dead.

On Halloween in Venice, almost two years after Mother rejected her humanity, I remembered her singing. I lit a candle for her. It wasn't for the seal or the selchie who had refused to become human again. I lit a candle for my human mother. The human who held me, signed to me, fought for me, danced for me. The human I yearned for every day. The human who was dead. In Venice, because of the crowds and the masks, you couldn't see anyone's face in the distance. They would be turning a corner just ahead of you and always out of reach. It was a fitting place to be haunted, especially by women. Whenever I thought of Mother or Neela, I would see them throughout the day, sometimes just a shoulder or an arm, other times their whole face, staring at me before rushing away.

❧

The day after Halloween, I stumbled out of my room around noon. I had spent a great portion of the night before with Petru and Zosia, watching slasher films and drinking red wine. It was the first time I saw Petru drink a lot. It made him quiet. His arm stayed around Zosia the entire night. Seeing them together comforted me. Impossible, really, after so much. He now told me about his other conquests freely, and I told him of mine. Knowing I may have helped him keep Zosia stirred a tingling under my skin. I made it all the way to the counter by the coffee pot before I noticed Father sitting out on the kitchen balcony holding what looked like a rusty knife with a red handle. I had never seen it before.

I poured coffee and walked over to him. His eyes were glazed, red-rimmed. His entire face seemed to be carrying a great weight. His hands gripped the knife. I now saw the small red cracked leather sleeve resting on Father's leg. I sat down on the empty black metal chair next to him, sipped my coffee, and waited. Hoping he would tell me a story.

He handed me the knife. *That's your grandfather's. You know he's dead, right?*

Yes. I remembered learning that when I was very young, but I never knew how or when. He had never told me.

That knife is all I have from him. It's a fishing knife. He was a fisherman. I have only a few memories of him. Do you want to know about this?

Yes. Of course I did. The coffee on the table was forgotten.

The first thing I remember is my father teaching me how to swim. We lived on a boat near Boston. He lifted me over the edge of our boat and threw me in the ocean. I gasped. Yeah. I had to learn fast. He was rough. I don't want to be harsh like him. He scared me but I do want to be strong like him. He taught me how to love the ocean. I swam with a giant sunfish one time, and I was terrified because I thought it was a shark. My father forced me to stay in the water. He told me to get close to it. I became fascinated because the sunfish was so huge, but it was so calm. It just floated around.

Once when I was five, I was swimming and my parents saw a shark below me. I didn't know. I couldn't see it. The shark was following me and it almost bit me. I thought they had imagined it but I remember my father's face so clearly. It was the only time he e-v-e-r looked scared.

Father's face had a shadow across it as he remembered. I wanted to reach my hand out and brush it away, but after a moment, I picked up my coffee instead.

DEPARTURE

I turned eighteen on a gondola ride with Zosia while drinking champagne. We were laughing at something the man paddling our boat had said to us when I thought of Mother and wanted to share something with Zosia. *My mother in Ireland refuses to see me because I like girls.*

Are you serious? That's ridiculous. I'm sorry but you obviously don't need her. Her smile faded to a frown.

But she's my mother. Sometimes I just can't deal with it.

Do you think my mother likes my choices? She hates that I live here and work on the streets. She thinks I'm wasting my life and I don't have a real job. Every time I visit her, she lectures me and we fight. That's why I don't go home much. Petru's parents are the same. You're not alone.

Mother's acceptance was never something I imagined I had to fight for until I lost it. I didn't realise it was something other people lived without, too. If it didn't even have to do with our being part animal, maybe it didn't matter that we were part animal after all. And if it didn't matter, maybe I really didn't need Mother as much as I thought I did. I wasn't a full selchie like her. I was human.

When I saw Mathi's face in the crowds by the Rialto, I thought I was imagining it. It wasn't until we made eye contact and he started towards me that I realised he was for real. He was in Venice, and I knew he had come here for me. I turned and zigzagged my way to Petru and Zosia's apartment. It was the only place where I knew he wouldn't find me.

I banged on the door until Zosia opened it.

What's wrong? Are you ok?

No. I signed as I sank down on one of the bar stools at their kitchen counter by the phone. *Can you call my father for me, please?*

Of course I will but what's the problem?

A boy from India is here. He chased me through the streets. He was my brother there but he wanted to marry me. He knows my address so I needed to come here. Please call my father and say M-a-t-h-i is here and he will soon show up at our apartment. Say that I am upset and I need him to tell M-a-t-h-i to go away and call back here when he leaves so I can go home and talk to my father. Ok?

As she picked up the phone, I lay my head down on the counter and closed my eyes while I waited. I couldn't believe he showed up immediately after I had finished school. I was still planning to fly to India. I hadn't bought my ticket yet, nor had I told Father about my plans. I put it off because he had just finished his novel and was busy looking for a research job in the Mediterranean, Indonesia, or Australia. He assumed I would go with him wherever he found work. I wasn't ready to tell him otherwise.

Zosia tapped me on the shoulder. When I raised my head, she signed, *Ok. Your father understands. He will do what you want him to do. Can you tell me more of the story, though? Can I help you any more?*

I adored her. She and Petru were my first friends. The kind of friends who you don't grow up and disappear from, the kind who remain close to you even if you live in different countries. Over cups of coffee and chocolate, I told her my story.

By the time I went home, it was late that night. Mathi had refused to leave immediately so Petru had to get him far enough away from my apartment for me to return without him seeing me. Father's face was downcast when I sat beside him on our couch.

Dad, I began, *before I left India, I promised Neela that I would return after I finished school. I wanted to tell you before but there was never a good time. I have enough money for the trip now. I have to go alone. I have to go before Mathi can follow me. I have to see Neela.*

I waited for him to respond but instead of signing, he stroked my hair. He had never touched me like that before. For a brief moment, I didn't want to go back. I imagined my life if I never went back to India and it felt okay.

I understand, he signed. *But Mathi told me something important. I don't want to hurt you but I must tell you. Neela is married now. I'm so sorry.* He touched my face gently, opening his arms for me to enter them, but I couldn't move. My world seemed to dissolve around me and my skin went numb. I couldn't feel his hand and I couldn't focus on his body sitting next to me. I stood up and went into my room and shut the door behind me.

My elephant sheets were in the back of my wardrobe. I dug them out, wrapped myself inside them, lay down on the floor, and sobbed.

INDIA

Palm: henna-covered, Neela's bangles dancing along the
wrist.

Black eyes: lined with black Eyetex, protection from sun,
beauty.

Silver rings: dark, cracked bare feet, three rings on each
second toe.

Gold-rimmed sari: caped around the face, shading
sunlight with itself.

Red: canyons leading into Earth, round pools, butterflies
landing, flying.

RED

My plane landed in Madras at nearly five am. I was home; back on red dirt, where all the brown men outside were trying to sell me taxi rides. There were dirty blue-rimmed local buses and rickshaws rumbling alongside the trash on the roads. I loved its pungency, the way it screamed out the reality of humanity, what we do to the Earth. Our footprints here were clearly marked, more real.

Women in purple saris hung around by the toilets pretending to clean and begging for money because *toilets clean right?* I smiled at them. Pressed rupees into their hands as I had never done before. It was worth it for me to see their wagging heads, their back-and-forth *yes*. Because I knew now that *yes* meant a lot of things.

The rising sun cast a red haze over the city. The warmth of the thick smoke-filled air wrapped around me, but I didn't sweat. I took a taxi to the bus station, and from there I found the local bus that led to my village, to *Ammā*, because I didn't know where Neela was. We couldn't ask Mathi. Father was busy tricking him into thinking that I was still in Venice so that I would have time to talk to her without the danger of Mathi trying to get me to marry him.

But the real danger was in a place no one could see. A place inside my newly positioned sari top over my heart that was now made of water. It soaked me. With each step I took, I was struggling to swim. Seeing Father's words over and over in the air before me: *Neela is married, Neela is married, Neela is married.* A haunting mantra that I wished was a lie.

I remembered every step of my journey as if I had never left. The palms along the beach where I learned how deep I was able to swim. We passed villagers herding goats and groups of boys holding long sticks. Temples painted in bright reds, blues and yellows, carved in the shapes of giant gods. The sea streaming in the background as I rode the bus down the coastal highway brought me back to the last morning I had spent with her.

❧

My eyes were dry when I woke to the blue dawn crawling in over the windowsill. Neela's still looked wet. The shock of leaving kept me contained. My emotions wrapped tight inside me, while the outside of me stayed numb. I kissed her awake. When her eyes opened, I signed, *Is it time to go now?*

She nodded as we dug for our saris and tops in the mess of sheets. Even the little elephants seemed to be screaming *staystaystay*, as they hid our clothes beneath their procession. Once dressed, we crept outside before anyone could see us and ran off towards the sea. I had told her I needed the sunrise. It was my last day in our village, on this coast, by this body of water. I didn't know that upon reaching it I would need to dive in. I grabbed her hand and ignored her protests. The sun hadn't yet climbed out of the waves and I wanted to find it below them. Swim to the sun beneath the surface with my love, carrying her. As Mother had once done for me.

Neela followed me tentatively, gasping as the water hit against her legs, hips, and chest. We had to hold our saris in place, too. No matter how the waves tried to push us down, or how our clothes dragged in the tides, Neela would not let go of my hand. It was new for me. Now *I* had the power. I could lead her through water like she had led me over the land.

We pushed past the waves until we couldn't touch the bottom anymore. I barely had to kick my feet below me to stay afloat, but Neela struggled to swim beside me. Her arms and legs flailed around her. I grabbed at her torso and held it close to my own. At first she panicked. She couldn't comprehend how my small form could possibly hold her afloat, until I started swimming far out towards the glow in the sky where the sun began to rise.

I turned to look into her eyes and the admiration I saw there changed me. My body felt stronger. My legs pumped as I rolled over on my back, holding Neela above me. It was easy. I tried lowering my head into the water. Neela struggled. I had to communicate something to her to get her to relax, but my hands were holding her. I raised my head again and mouthed, *Stop, trust me.*

She let her body go slack and I was able to try it again. I lowered my head back into the water just below the surface. The world was upside-down, but I was able to see far below us and ahead. Schools of fish flashed in the distance. We passed the *kathu maram*, the canoe-like fishing boats with triangular sails. They were beautiful when they rode the waves at dawn.

After a few minutes I realised something else about my body: my nose was different. I felt a piece of flesh inside my nostrils close so that water didn't enter my nose as my head hung below the surface, like a seal's nose. I lifted my head back out to find Neela staring at me. She looked terrified, curious, and shocked all at once. I slowed down. We were far out past the boats, closer to the sun, but it had risen up out of the sea before we were able to reach it. All we could do was swim back. I began to get tired when we reached the breaking waves, but by then Neela was able to manage herself. Men along the edges of my vision were staring at us.

We sat in the sand. Our soaked bodies quickly became covered in tiny yellow stones and bits of shells. Neela was gasping for breath. Her hands trembled as she signed, *How did you do that? You swam too far and was underwater for too long! You're crazy!*

I never told you that my mother is part s-e-a-l. She lives in the sea. Look at my hands.

I spread my fingers so that she could see the webs better. Neela: believer of demons, monsters, thousands of gods. She was having trouble with this? I could see in her eyes that her mind was fighting with itself. It didn't make sense to me. She had experienced it! What was there to dispute?

After a few long minutes she said, *Maybe you were possessed by a sea demon?*

What? No, no, it's part of me. It's just me.

I don't know. I don't understand. Let's go home and get dry?

I reached out to embrace her, but she pulled away sharply. Her reaction cut me and almost brought me to tears. I wanted to be her heroine. I thought she would think it was beautiful, or good, not this confusion, this fear. Where was the glimpse of admiration I saw out in the water? A trick of the dawn. Mirage. Illusion. Dream.

I wished I were a ghost or a mermaid. I wanted to disappear like a myth back into the sea, but I couldn't. I had to lift up my wet skirts and trudge back to our house beside my lover who seemed much happier to have me leave her in a few hours. Tears suddenly came. I suppose I should have been grateful that, upon seeing them, Neela forgot her fears about my existence and embraced me. I felt worse as I melted into her. Whatever power the sea gave me was gone.

The bus rocked. The little boy next to me sat on his mother's lap, large brown eyes staring at me, taking me in, frowning because I was frowning. I tried to smile for him. He giggled, reached out towards my hair, but his mother grabbed his hand, pulled it down, and kept her gaze steady ahead.

I looked out the window at the orange streets and bright green leaves. The red canyons: where things began, ended, and began again. Circles. There were no lines anywhere. A Universe of curves. We had to lean this way or that to adapt.

I arrived dusty. My blue sari trailed a little too much along the dirt. I carried my bags up the street that used to be mine, past the shop where we had bought coconuts. They were piled up in round brown clusters, bananas hanging in groups, mangoes in piles. I wanted to sit in the plastic chairs, sip chai while watching the passing street traffic, pet the stray dogs, and laugh at the goats. But I couldn't pause. I felt Kali walking beside me, her red sari trailing behind us. Kali's passion burned within me. I could be red here, too. My auburn hair reached my waist. I felt like a proper Indian woman with long hair hanging down my back. Kali was my sister. I walked to the house I knew so well.

Ammā was sweeping the front step for what was probably the thousandth time that day. I could barely tell she was older. She threw the broom aside when she saw me. Her hands flew to her face. She screamed as only *Ammā* could scream. I smiled as we embraced each other fiercely. It nearly broke my resolve, but I held myself together. She began babbling in Tamil. I caught a word or two here and there. She pulled me inside for tea. I was sad to see that Ariyan was gone. It seemed Neela had taken him.

She ranted for a while to my deaf ears, grabbed a photograph, and pushed it into my face. It was Neela in a ceremonial dress and so much make-up, so much red, decorated with white jasmine flowers. I didn't care about the man at her shoulder, who, like most Indians, was incapable of smiling in a photo. I just cared that she was smiling. Her happiness infuriated me. *Ammā* told me that Neela lived in Pondy and she would love to see me. *Would I go now to see her? Yes.* Yes, I would. I couldn't stay here. Had to get to *her*. I clutched the tiny silver Ganesh at my throat, wishing.

I carried my bags back down the street, heading for the bus that would lead me to Pondy. Less than an hour, another taxi, and I would be there. I barely noticed the palm forests I passed through, temples, tea shops, and villages. I showed the taxi driver a paper with the directions and we were off.

We pulled up at a small white house down a dirt road from a crowded street. I walked through a gate on the side and around to the back door. I felt years of hunger welling up inside me. Ariyan rushed outside leaping and barking. Once he smelled me, he became overjoyed the way only dogs could be, licking as much of me as he could find, pushing his head up under my sari skirt and into my arms, against my neck, as I bent down. He managed to be everywhere as if he had a thousand heads rather than one.

I watched her bare feet step out of the door. Rows of silver toe rings shone in the sunlight. Three on each second toe, the place of wives. She wore a yellow sari, just yellow, no patterns. A blur of sun. Her face was rounder. Her dark eyes were lined in black. Perfect lips I just wanted—

We rushed to each other at the same time. She was finally in my arms. Her body hard and soft. Silky fabric tangled in my hands. My face buried itself in her neck. Home. Nothing else was home like this. She stepped back too soon. Her eyes searched beyond me as she signed, *Where's Mathi? I thought he brought you.*

Mathi's awful. He wants to marry me but has no respect for me. He chased me. It was wrong of him. She had to understand, but instead she looked hurt.

We just want you back. She signed with perfect fluency as if she had never stopped. *You're part of our family. I want you to marry Mathi.*

What about you? I came back for you, not Mathi! I don't want a man. I want you.

But we can't get married. It's not ok here, and here is my home.

And you're already married. My hands trembled.

Yes. I wanted to tell you. I want you to be here with me. Her hands reached out, but I couldn't let them touch me. Her words already cut too deep.

But I was coming back! I would have taken you away to a place where we can marry each other and be together. Do you even love me anymore? Or do you love a man instead?

My universe hung in the balance upon her answer. I waited as if standing on a rope far up in the clouds. She ushered me into a bedroom decorated almost identical to our old room. There was a picture of Ganesh on the wall above the area set up for *puja*. She shut the door and turned to me. The weight she gained made her so much fuller, more alive. She pulled me into the folds of her beauty, my face against her breasts. I didn't want to be anywhere else in the world.

She guided me down upon the bed and kissed me in a way that felt different than any other kiss we ever had. It wasn't fierce or soft, but something that had deepened with age. I knew then that she had been thinking of me, missed me, wanted me. I couldn't follow all the stories her lips told me. My skin gathered them up and stored them inside. The soft curtain of her dark hair was around me, mixing with mine. They were black and red with passion between.

Eventually, she pulled away and the world snapped us back to the room. Ganesh on the wall. A breeze wandered in through the open window.

Banana palms outside instead of papaya trees. Her hands moved, in that graceful way that only her hands could do. *Of course, I love you. Please always remember that I love you most. More than any man, more than me, more than Ammā, more than Ganesh! But I can't leave my home. I can't be with you. I'm pregnant now and I'm having my child here. There's no other way.*

I had to grip her arms to steady myself. Everything was caving in. The walls. The bed. I saw Ganesh falling forward and multiplying into a thousand elephants rushing across our sheets. My sheets. I wanted to hide. Become something she could stick into her breasts forever. Tiny. Hers. Against her skin, always.

But how can you do this if you love me? How could you let him give you a child? That should be our child! I managed to say.

How can you give me a child? How else can I have a child?

In the West, there are ways. We don't need men.

But this is India. The world is different here. I'm not Western like you. I'm Indian! I thought you were happy here with me. I thought you were Indian, too.

Happy in a place where I can only touch you in secret? Where we have to marry men? How can I be happy here?

We cried, tried to reach for each other, but our words crowded the air between us, pushing us apart. I couldn't touch her in secret anymore. The air was too thick. She laid her head down on my lap, between my thighs. I touched her like something foreign. Tracing the silvery edges of a ghost. A beautiful mirage, yellow, like the sun, but the red swallowed us. Spilled us out like blood. Waters of the heart—red, staining.

ROOTS

I left Neela in tears and boarded the train that would take me the farthest south. I was ready for the sea. Kanyakumari. The southernmost tip of India. The place where the three oceans merged: the Arabian Sea, the Indian Ocean, and the Bay of Bengal. Crowds mingled all around me in this place of pilgrimage, this auspicious meeting point of the three seas. Mostly Indian tourists came here. They came to watch the sun set and rise out of water. It was one of the only places in the world where you could watch the sun rise out of one sea and set into another while standing in the same place. A Gandhi Memorial was here, too, among others. An island of rock just beyond the tip stood alone in the waves.

I sat on the steps by the waters, a small human in a crowd of hundreds facing the setting sun. People watched it like they had never seen a sunset before. Great ball of yellow turned pink, coral, orange, red. It felt like another world, a world where here, this, was my first sunset. The end of the first day. I sat against a stone wall beside steps leading into the sea. The sun's red ball dipped into the distant blue. I closed my eyes. I wanted quiet space. I wanted to be cold like Mother or a creature like *makara*, a water beast, a hybrid monster ridden by a god, because I had been. Ridden by Neela, who was just as powerful as Parvati or Kali. Ridden by a sun so hot she burned my skin until I was a monster, too. Already in-between. *Bhí mé idir eatarthu.*

I only wanted to be one or the other.

Above the deep blue lapping waves of the sea, I saw my namesake rising up—Lakshmi. She rode a great owl as she held a lotus flower in one of her four arms coiled down like a snake through the ripples, along the steps, towards me. It felt both soft and hard when it touched my feet. She smiled. I noticed her skin—white—the colour of her as Mother Earth.

My roots. The lotus. The banyan. The Mother India. With my hands against the stones, I could almost feel through the Earth, the Alps on the other side, the islands of Venice, the cliffs by the sea in *Dún Chaoin*. Connection. I could touch the Earth from any side. The memories of my life were stories, and these stories were my roots. I felt them as I followed the dark streets with my eyes, the echo of my thoughts vibrating like the black shadows that once crawled over the buildings. But these shadows were warm. My past spreading out, embracing the larger, darker shadow of India above me, as I rested against her tip, her bottom edge where the sea and the sun kissed her every night and day.

I sat there through the dark. People kept moving around. I could smell the various street foods being cooked throughout the night. Fried chickpea flour in the air. As it got closer to sunrise, I smiled at the unmistakable scent of idli being steamed.

I sat there against the stone. Waiting for the sun to swim through the sea and rise up on the other side. I wanted to take my sari off. Unravel. Step into the ocean. Swim out to meet it. But Lakshmi stood in my way with her owl-wisdom, keeping me at peace despite empty feelings, anger, jealousy.

As the sky turned from violet to lavender, to pale gold, yellow, pink, I felt my rage slip away into the dark waters. Sink down along the steps, towards the bottom of the sea where it belonged. I watched the distant waves, suddenly remembering the rest of Father's story of my grandfather's death:

I was young, maybe eight or nine. My father decided he wanted to go A-l-a-s-k-a-n crab fishing. It's the most dangerous fishing in the world. Boats always sink. The waves are huge and the water is frozen. There are countless storms and everything is harsh and cold but my father loved that. He didn't care about the money. He only cared about the sea. My mother said if he left she would divorce him. He went anyway. He said he would see me soon. One month later, we heard his ship sank. Do you know what my father did? He tied himself to the boat. He must have known he was dying and it was the only way his body would be found.

The ocean had stolen so much—Mother, my grandfather, Neela's father. Yet Father hated to leave it, and I had spent most of my life trying to swim, trying to stay by it, in it, with Mother. We were sea creatures. I suddenly missed Father. I had spent all my time focused on *her*, on Neela, or on Mother, while he was there—waiting. I couldn't make him wait any longer.

ॐ

Sunrise.

It looked grander over these seas, stuck revolving around this tiny world of humans and violence and love and mutations, like me. Stuck in the sky like Neela was stuck on land, and me struggling to swim in the sand, realising that I had branches and roots as well as webbed fingers.

The sun stayed intact. Shining new every morning. We always want what we can *almost* have. Neela was stolen but somehow it didn't stop the sun from rising. Brilliantly red, orange, yellow. Rounded fire. Dark faces watching, rapt. As if they had never seen the sun. To my right there were women and men bathing, half-soaked in these sacred waters.

As I watched the women holding the weight of their wet saris in their hands like eels in the shades of blue, purple, brown, I realised I could step into these waters, dive past Lakshmi standing guard. Dive into the unfeeling sea. Meet my grandfather in that world beneath the waves. I could swim until my arms were tired. Until my own sari pulled me down down down. I felt power in that knowledge. It tasted metallic like copper, it looked like Kali, scythe in her hands, skulls across her breasts, mouths agape. I could stick my tongue out. I could be red like the sun, smothered by the sea. And I could know that it wasn't the sea that chose me. *I* could choose. I could choose something other than life.

The sun, a warning of every dawn I would miss, blinded me. Every body I would never touch. A memory pushing through the rays of light as I sat balanced on the edge of India, much like I once balanced in that Venetian courtyard staring at the red-haired man across the stone, my branches shaking, wanting—I wanted to be found, I just hadn't wanted it to be him. Father—

Here: Kanyakumari dawning, rising out of the sea. The women bathing around me, splashing these triune waters, smiling into my eyes, wagging heads side-to-side. My eyes tearing from the brightness—

I dipped my webbed toes into the waves.

The waters swallowed me.

Turquoise and deep blue chased me down into the deep, past the soft ankles of women, the tiny silver bangles and toe rings they wore. I reached for sharp coral, shiny edges of fish, steps descending and disappearing into sand. My sari moved like eelgrass. It didn't tear or stick. Something called me deeper. Towards my grandfather's shipwreck, his body twisted up in ropes, falling apart with each motion of the sea. I swam hard like a seal, like I had never been human. Grandfather. No. *Father.* He was here, somewhere. I felt his body encased in waves, swallowing, swallowing him. *But he can't breathe like us!* I screamed to no one in particular. Everything was deaf down here. Every sea the same thick water body swallowing sound, swallowing humans, filling their lungs with water instead of air. *Why isn't she with him?* Mother wouldn't be his saviour. No. In Ireland, I must have imagined her. She wasn't there. She didn't help to save him. I just wanted her to because he was supposed to be hers. Wasn't he? I tore through the liquid world, aiming northwest, aiming for the Red Sea. It can't be that far. I swam like I never did before. I swam until the waters turned green and the sun set and rose again. Days without air. I swam until Neela caught up with me. She wrapped around my leg like a moray eel. *Squeeze me,* I begged her with my hands in between strokes. *Take me. Hold me. Keep me. Have me. Don't let me go.* I signed with fervour to the fish. A whale shark up ahead had a gaping mouth. I wanted to dive into it. Lose myself in the muscles of something larger. Something that would embrace me without question. Without judgment. *Father.* Not Mother. Not Mum. *Dad.* He was a sea creature, too. Wasn't he? The school of yellow and black fish tickled my ankles as they passed in bursts, not sure if I was part of the sea or not. Like Casanova chasing me down a Venetian street as I chased Petru and Zosia. The lovers. The lovers just ahead, always. Would *I* ever find a lover like that? Neela haunted me with each passing wave, each bubble reminder of the air above. Reminder of wind and storms. Neela ripped from me like a storm. She was coral: rock hard and sharp yet delicate. I smelled the salt of her tears, her sweat. That smooth, dark body beside me. Sex that had felt like the cracking open of a universe, a door ripping between this word and another, and we passed through. We swam into the place where Kali smiled her red lust grin, her tongue dancing like a Venetian mime swaying on the pavement, a fiery reminder of passion. Passion we couldn't keep. It tore ahead of us—a fish darting away, driven by its own means, driven by something we were barely able to touch. Sometimes love was like the door to a magical realm where humans and animals and gods roamed together, harmonious, but we were always stopped at the entrance. Never able to pass through completely, but every time, every kiss, every fingertip, we were closer to it. If you touched the door enough times, it drove you mad. Father must have known that, but he kept swimming up to it, too. He returned. Didn't he? The sea told me how they lied—ravenously, as passionate as their love, I was certain. I swam with renewed trust that she was there. She did save him. She carried him through the door into the land where they could live under the sea in a castle of rock with sponge beds. I swam until I saw nothing but my father swimming ahead of me, just out of reach. *Dad!* I screamed with hands, with lips, with my outstretched arms and my webbed fingers spread wide. He was there, wasn't he? In the castle under the sea with the selchies, with mermaids and mermen and all the things we've only read about in books. Stories with a taste that stayed in your mouth, a scent you could never forget, that you smelled even in water. Through liquid, passion called me. Passion howled and the fish cleared a path that sparkled with tiny scales. The silver dust of childlike dreams. A need so great it was unquenchable. Love was for children, wasn't it? Not something adults could ever understand, even if they swallowed it whole like an oyster with a pearl that cracks open when it passes our hearts, cracks open and bleeds its light into our bodies—we shatter. Love always turns things inside out. I swam hard like a seal, like I had never been human. I loved hard, loved like I had always been human, wanting him even when I didn't know I wanted him. Wanting him with the love of a child, because I didn't have that love as a child. *Dad!* I said to the ship's hulls gliding above me, reminding me of what he was before I had been born, before I spent my life distracted from him, enraptured by the colour of each sari she wore against her skin, the silk that shone like the scales of a fish in the deep, hypnotising me while his pen wrote, while his fingers typed in a language of love I hadn't known he knew. A language of doors to other worlds, places where humans and animals, deafness and hearing, male and female, were all woven together in a tapestry of passion where things were the same because they weren't the same. Where love was wind and water and the spaces in between and passion breathed fire cool enough to touch, warm enough to cradle within our thousand arms, one for each god each wave of the ocean. My father was a door at the bottom of the sea and I swam hard like a seal towards him. I swam hard, but where? Where was he now? I felt eelgrass and other seals, not the bottoms of gondolas. Not canals. I swam until it hurt. I swam because I wasn't sure if he was swimming anymore. My arms grew heavy and my legs felt like they were kicking through tar. *This wasn't supposed to happen!* I shouted at the nearest fish, a catfish with long whiskers, ignoring me. Maybe I wasn't a seal after all. Maybe I really couldn't be *her.* I felt him slipping from me. *Dad!* I screamed and the water entered my throat. I coughed and more water flooded my mouth, my lungs. I wanted to drown. Wanted to give up. Wanted to open that door at the bottom of the sea—the door that had to lead me to *him.* I struggled and pushed, cupping water in claw-like hands, fingers cracking from the pressure. *But I'm a seal!* I screamed and the sea screamed back. The waves tossed me around like a cork bobbing up towards the surface because I wasn't supposed to be so far down. There was no such thing as a seal wearing a sari or a girl with webbed hands, was there? I swam hard like a girl. Like a human. I pushed myself through the white foam like I was pushing through the loss of them all—Mother, Neela, Father—they stuck to me like my sari. The weight of them all began to pull my tired body down but I kept pushing—towards another door, another chance to feel the softness of a woman's arm against mine. Even if I didn't yet believe it. Didn't yet want anyone except Neela. No. I wasn't ready to drown either. I pulled myself upwards, climbing towards the brightness of the sun's rays streaming through the water above me, wishing I had made it—wishing I would see *an fear marbh* when I reached the surface but knowing in my heart that India would still be there on the horizon. Turquoise and green waters parted. I broke through the surf, mouth agape, spilling water. The air entered me quickly, as if it were taking back its rightful place within my body. It tasted like the sun.

GLOSSARY

Tamil:

ammā: mother
nandre: thank you
punjabi: type of dress consisting of loose pants and a long tunic short
or long-sleeved top with a scarf; technically known as *salwar kameez* or
punjabi suit, but commonly called *punjabi*
puja: a Sanskrit word meaning worship or adoration; it is done in
temples as well as in the home, where a space is often set aside where
people pray and leave offerings of flowers to small effigies of gods

Irish:

A athair: father
An Blascaod Mór: the Great Blasket Island
An bhrúch: selchie
An Fear Marbh: The Dead Man
An fharraige: the sea
A Mháthair: mother
An Tiaracht: Tearaght Island
Ar na tonnta: on the waves
Inis Mhic Uileáin: an Irish saint's name
Más é do thoil é: please
Na Blascaodaí: the Blasket Islands
Na hOileáin: the islands
Raghaimíd: let's go
Bhí mé idir eatarthu: I am in between
Tráigh a' Choma: Coumeenole Beach

ACKNOWLEDGMENTS

This book could never have happened without my experiences at Goddard College's MFA program in Plainfield, Vermont. I deeply send my thanks out to every student and every faculty member I grew to know and love from 2006-2008 while at Goddard (there are too many of you to name).

Some specific people whose editorial advice was invaluable in the crafting of these pages were: Bhanu Kapil, Kenny Fries, Elena Georgiou, K. L. Pereira, Jennifer Smith, Kristen Harmon, and John Lee Clark.

I'd like to thank the following people for their friendship and support through the writing of these pages: Rob Lusignan, Kat Good-Schiff, Daniel Heacox, Chad Dean, Thirza Defoe, Patrick Kieffer, Judie Gonsalves, Anthony DiPietro, Lauren Winterholer, Mindy Barrett, Pearl Gittins, and my mother, Shirley Ringman.

I beg forgiveness of anyone I have forgotten to mention.

I couldn't have begun to write about these myths or characters without my experiences living in Tamil Nadu of South India and Co. Kerry of Ireland, and the time I spent in Venice doing some emotional healing and processing of my own.

Lastly, I offer up oceans of gratitude to Raymond Luczak for his passionate faith in *Makara* that has allowed it to manifest in the form it has taken.

ABOUT THE AUTHOR

Kristen Ringman grew up in Rhode Island with a deaf mother and gradually went deaf herself by her early 20s. She attended the University of New Hampshire for her undergraduate studies and spent the next few years working with stray dogs in South India, volunteering with Peace Corps Kenya's Deaf Education program, and teaching mural painting at a primary school in Ireland. She received her MFA in Creative Writing from Goddard College in 2008.

Her poetry, fiction, and creative nonfiction have appeared in *Deaf American Prose: 1980 to 2010*, *Deaf American Poetry: An Anthology*, *Eyes of Desire 2: A Deaf GLBT Reader*, and other anthologies and literary journals. In August 2011 she received a fellowship to attend AROHO Women's Writing Retreat at Ghost Ranch in New Mexico where she taught a Barefoot Walking Meditation class and gave a presentation called "Through the Lens of Deafness and Other Disabilities."

She spent a few years living on sailboats and sailing between Block Island, RI and Key West, FL. She is currently working on an urban fantasy saga about a wolf girl. She lives in New Hampshire with her family and her Hearing service dog with a goal of sailing around the world someday.

www.kristenringman.com

ABOUT THE PUBLISHER

Handtype Press is a company that showcases the finest literature created by signers, Deaf and hearing alike, or about the Deaf or signing experience the world over. Our titles include John Lee Clark's anthology *Deaf Lit Extravaganza* and Kristen Ringman's *Makara: A Novel*.

In addition to focusing on the Deaf community, Handtype Press maintains a separate imprint called Squares & Rebels focusing on LGBT writers with a strong Midwestern connection. Squares & Rebels has published two anthologies: Kate Lynn Hibbard's *When We Become Weavers: Queer Female Poets on the Midwestern Experience* and Raymond Luczak's *Among the Leaves: Queer Male Poets on the Midwestern Experience*.

www.handtype.com

www.squaresandrebels.com

CPSIA information can be obtained at www.ICGtesting.com
Printed in the USA
BVOW081502131212

308154BV00014B/158/P

MAR 0 7 2013

only copy in system